FULL WOLF MOON

DOUBLEDAY

NEW YORK

LONDON

TORONTO

SYDNEY

AUCKLAND

FULL WOLF MOON

· A NOVEL ·

LINCOLN CHILD

Copyright © 2017 by Lincoln Child

All rights reserved. Published in the United States by Doubleday, a division of Penguin Random House LLC, New York, and distributed in Canada by Random House of Canada, a division of Penguin Random House Canada Limited, Toronto.

www.doubleday.com

DOUBLEDAY and the portrayal of an anchor with a dolphin are registered trademarks of Penguin Random House LLC.

Jacket design by Michael J. Windsor
Jacket illustrations: cabin © swa182 / Shutterstock; moon © Suppakij1017 / Shutterstock; forest © Gallinago media / Shutterstock, PlusONE / Shutterstock, Bildagentur Zoonar GmbH / Shutterstock

Library of Congress Cataloging-in-Publication Data

Names: Child, Lincoln, author.
Title: Full wolf moon : a novel / Lincoln Child.
Description: First edition. | New York : Doubleday, [2017]
Identifiers: LCCN 2017002292 | ISBN 9780385531429 (hardback) | ISBN 9780385531436 (ebook)
Subjects: LCSH: Paranormal fiction. | Suspense fiction. | BISAC: FICTION / Action & Adventure. | FICTION / Suspense.
Classification: LCC PS3553.H4839 F85 2017 | DDC 813/.54—dc23
LC record available at https://lccn.loc.gov/2017002292

MANUFACTURED IN THE UNITED STATES OF AMERICA

1 3 5 7 9 10 8 6 4 2

First Edition

To Veronica

FULL WOLF MOON

(FULL WOLF MOON. The name once associated by the Algonquin Indians with the full moon of January, when the wolf packs were hungry and howled close to Native American villages.)

1

At seven thirty in the evening Palmer stopped for another snack—handmade gorp and an energy bar from the lid pocket of his backpack. He'd sworn hours before that he wouldn't allow himself a real dinner—hot and steaming from his titanium griddle—until he'd found a decent place to tent for the night.

He looked around slowly as he chewed the energy bar. He'd known it would be a rough slog, and he had believed himself familiar with the surrounding region, but nothing had prepared him for the hike in that day. *Guess all the stories were true,* he thought a little sourly.

It was the second weekend in July, the sun was just starting to slip behind the horizon to the west, but he could nevertheless make out Desolation Mountain, maybe four miles to the north.

It stood there, alone, a mirror of blue-black lake at its base, its green flanks exposed as if taunting him. Four miles—but with this country, it might as well be forty.

"Shit," he muttered, shoving the wrapper of the energy bar into his pocket and starting off once again.

Desolation Mountain was a trailless peak of 3,250 feet, making it not high enough to be among the "true" forty-six Adirondack tall peaks. Even so, its vertical rise and distance from other summits made it worth notching his belt with. But what made the mountain most attractive to hard-core backpackers, mountain hikers, and students of the Adirondacks was its remoteness. It was situated in the Desolation Lake area, west of the Five Ponds Wilderness—perhaps the wildest, most remote section of the entire six-million-acre park.

Remoteness didn't bother David Palmer. He liked nothing better than to disappear into the wilderness and go for days without seeing another human being. It was actually getting to the mountain that was proving a real bitch.

At first, it hadn't been bad at all. He'd left his SUV hidden among the trees at the Baldwin Mountain trailhead, then hiked five miles down a private logging road until at last it petered out. This was followed by miles of virgin, old-growth timber, so tall that it was always dusk beneath and the forest floor was soft and completely free of saplings.

But then he left the Five Ponds Wilderness, the forest fell away behind him, and he began the approach to Desolation Lake. And here was where his fast, easy pace suddenly slowed to a crawl. The country grew ugly, barren, and nearly impossible to traverse. The wilderness between him and the mountain became a labyrinth of outwash bogs, blowdowns, and "kettle holes," forcing him to watch every step he took. There was no trail, of course, not even a herd path, and with ravines running at crisscrosses to each other he'd had to rely frequently on his Garmin Oregon handheld GPS. More than once he'd slipped on treacherous, barely visible rocks covered with lichen. Thank God he'd decided on wearing his off-trail boots—otherwise he'd have turned an ankle, or worse, long before now.

After another quarter mile, he stopped again. The way ahead was blocked by an overlapping downfall too tight for him to squeeze through with the heavy pack on his back. Cursing under his breath, he shrugged out of the pack, found the widest hole in the downfall, shoved the pack through, then wiggled his way in behind it. The dry ends of branches poked at his limbs and scratched his face.

On the far side of the downfall he put the pack back on, making sure that the compression straps were good and tight. This late in the day a pack began to get heavy, and he wanted to make sure its contents stayed stable.

He spent a moment, shrugging his shoulders this way and that, getting the pack into position. Even though the majority of hikers used internal backpacks these days, Palmer still preferred one with an external frame—in his case, a Kelty Tioga. He tended to travel heavy, and he found externals easier not only to pack, but to carry and balance as well.

The sun had disappeared, and the landscape was growing darker by the minute. The change was actually perceptible to him, as if some god of nature was slowly turning down the dimmer switch. A full moon was rising into the black sky, lending a strange, dappled, almost spectral luminescence to the landscape, but he wasn't going to rely on the moonlight: it had the tendency to camouflage things, hiding sinkholes and gullies, and he'd learned the hard way not to trust to chance. He reached for the flashlight clipped to his belt, plucked it off, and turned it on.

By now it was past nine. As he started off again, he did a mental calculation and determined his pace had slowed to something like half a mile an hour. Of course, he could keep going until he reached Desolation Lake and camp on the shore. But he wouldn't get there until at least midnight, and by that time he'd be too whipped for an enjoyable climb the next day. No: there had to be a spot, *some* spot, in this godforsaken wilderness flat and bare enough for him to pitch his three-season tent and spread out his cookware. A hot meal, a soft sleeping bag, were beginning to seem like unattainable luxuries.

Not for the first time, as he made his way carefully forward, flashlight beam licking this way and that, he wished that he was back in the High Peaks region of the park. True, the trails there were often as wide as superhighways, and you were always tripping over other hikers, but at least you had a regular, goddamn forest around you with clearings and glades, not this alien riot of—

He stopped by a cluster of witch-hobble. He'd been so absorbed in his thoughts, and in his perusal of the treacherous ground ahead of him, that he hadn't realized there was a strange smell in the air. He sniffed. It was faint, but discernible: sour, a little musky; not skunklike exactly but definitely unpleasant.

Palmer shone his light around, but there was nothing. He shrugged and continued.

The moon was rising higher in the sky, bathing Desolation Mountain in its lambent glow. Three miles left. Hell, maybe he should just try to bushwhack his way to the lake, after all. But then there was the trip back to consider, and he had to—

There it was again: that smell. It was stronger now, and fouler: rank and animal.

Once again he stopped and searched around with his flashlight, feeling a prickle of anxiety this time. Small saplings and a latticework of flattened, fallen tree limbs reflected the beam back at him. The bright circle of light made everything outside it pitch-black.

Palmer shook his head. He was letting the eerie desolation of this place get to him. He'd barely seen an animal all day, just a single raccoon and a couple of young foxes. And that had been back in the old-growth forest. No animal in its right mind larger than a mouse would live in this kind of shit. His frustrating slog had to end sooner or later. And once he had a bellyful of chili inside him and his favorite inflatable air mattress beneath his sleeping bag, he'd be—

Now the smell was back, worse than ever, and with it came a sound—a deep, guttural noise, half grunt, half snarl. It sounded angry—angry and hungry.

Without even pausing to think, Palmer began to run. He ran as fast as the heavy pack allowed, the flashlight beam striping crazily ahead of him, panting, gasping, bounding over fallen trees and kettle holes, as the grunting and snuffling grew increasingly loud behind him.

And then his foot snagged on a protruding root; he crashed heavily to the ground; a heavy weight that had nothing to do with his pack pressed suddenly against his back—a horrible, rending pain like nothing he'd experienced in his life clawed across his face and neck as the reek washed over him like a wave, then another explosion of pain, then still another . . . and then everything faded, first to red, and then to black.

2

THREE MONTHS LATER

From the suburbs of New Haven, the route led north to Water-bury, then west along the meandering line of I-84 until—after it crossed into New York State and passed over the Newburgh-Beacon Bridge—it intersected with I-87, the New York Thruway. Here the route became much more direct, arrowing north until the low, furred peaks of the Catskills began to assert themselves to the left. Traffic on this Friday afternoon grew heavier as Albany approached. It thinned out somewhat at Glens Falls, where all the trailers and flatbeds carrying Formula One vehicles bound for Watkins Glen exited. It thinned even further at Lake George, which even this late in the year drew tourists and weekending families.

It was at the first rest stop after Lake George that Jeremy Logan pulled over his vintage Lotus Elan and—although the afternoon was lengthening and the temperature hovering just above sixty—stopped long enough to put the roadster's top down before proceeding.

It had been fifteen years since he'd last made this journey, but this last part had always been his favorite leg and he was determined to enjoy it. With each passing town—Pottersville, Schroon Lake, North Hudson—the traffic lessened and the mountains around him swelled as if heaved up from the ground. The dark bulks of the High Peaks of the Adirondacks rose skyward, proud and inviolate, clad in their October hues of green and russet and gold, dwarfing the Catskills he'd traveled through not three hours before. The air that rushed past his windscreen became deliciously cool, freighted with the smell of pine. The setting sun gilded the bald tops of the taller mountains, while the valleys and cols between them—thick with spruce, beech, and birch—grew ever darker and more mysterious.

The Northway—as this section of I-87 was called—was as scarred and seamed with tar sealant as he'd always remembered, and with a little imagination he could relive the last time he'd made this drive, with John Coltrane and Bill Evans just barely audible on the half-muted stereo and Karen, his wife, sitting in the passenger seat. There was something about the ever-increasing height and bulk of the surrounding mountains, the afterglow and fast-onrushing night, that always seemed to coincide with the last leg of the six-hour drive from Connecticut, that quickened his pulse and whetted a taste for adventure.

Logan had never been much of an outdoors type—he'd been a passable fly fisherman as a youth, taught by a father with a mania for the sport, and he could usually manage to finish eighteen holes of golf with a score of less than three digits. But he had no patience for such things as jogging or running marathons—such activities seemed paralyzingly dull to him, a hamster running in its wheel. But one long weekend early into his marriage, another couple who were both assistant professors at Yale and card-carrying AMC members had convinced him and Kit to come along for a climb up Whiteface Mountain, just north of Lake Placid. Logan had accepted with reservations, only to find the mini-vacation a delight. There was something deeply satisfying about hiking up a mountain—selecting a route, navigating the trail blazes, enjoying the beauty of the changing microclimate as you ascended, pacing yourself for the truly steep stretches . . . and then at last breaking through the tree line and following the meandering rock cairns to the summit itself. Not only were the views remarkable, but there was something ineffably rewarding about conquering the peak itself. No, that wasn't right, because these mountains could not be conquered, or even tamed—it was more like coming to an accommodation, an understanding, with them. It was something you could never get from a treadmill session. After Whiteface, he and his wife had returned again, several years in a row, becoming modest "peak baggers": Algonquin, Cascade, Porter, Giant, and of course Mount Marcy—at 5,344 feet the tallest mountain in New York State.

But then their careers—his as a scholar-professor and hers as a professional cellist—had increasingly taken over their time. And what vacations they had were taken up with trips abroad to supplement his research, or to spend a week at Tanglewood when Karen was playing at the music festival there—and the three-day weekends in the High Peaks fell away behind them, just as the Northway was doing now in his rearview mirror.

At Underwood, he turned off the interstate onto NY 73 and followed the road as it wandered through thick forests and past fierce waterspouts rushing down stony gorges. He drove through Keene Valley and the town of Keene itself, then arrowed directly westward for Lake Placid and, beyond it, the village of Saranac Lake. The towns were a little larger than he remembered, and on their verges the footprint of man cut a little more heavily into the forest, but the changes were subtle and he remained irresistibly reminded of trips past.

"It's almost the same, Kit," he said as he drove. "It's like our last trip up, when we climbed Skylight and almost got lost in the fog."

He often found himself talking to Kit, dead of cancer now for more than five years. Naturally he did this only when he was by himself—save for Kit, of course—and yet it was less of a one-way conversation than one might have expected.

At Saranac Lake, he turned left onto Route 3, heading in the direction of Tupper Lake. Only the occasional car passed him now in the other direction, headlights winking in the humid forest air. He was not as familiar with this part of the park and—with an intense darkness closing in around him—he drove more slowly. About five miles farther on, his headlights illuminated a large, open gate cut into the thick spruce forest to his right. There was no signage on or beside the gate, merely a large metal symbol: a cumulus cloud hovering over a rippling watery surface.

He turned in, followed a bumpy, heavily rutted dirt road for perhaps two thousand feet—and then, suddenly, the forest parted to reveal a vast, weathered, three-storied structure of dark brown wood and rough-hewn stone. It sat beneath a massive, shingled

A-frame roof in Swiss chalet style that went from the serried chimneys along its ridge vent almost all the way to the ground. Twigwork balconies ran along the entire second floor as well as the third, shorter floor, and from within the large, red-framed windows that stood in series, the welcome glow of countless lamps and fireplaces beckoned.

This was Cloudwater, Logan's destination. But it had not always been known by that name. Sixty years before, it had been Rainshadow Lodge: one of the "Great Camps" built in the late nineteenth century as summer residences of the very rich along the lake shores of wild corners in upstate New York and New England. And Rainshadow Lodge, with its quintessential "Adirondack Rustic" architecture and huge cupolaed boathouse situated on Rainshadow Lake, had been one of the most famous and grandiose of all.

But all that had changed in 1954. Now its function was to serve as far more than just an oversized rustic summer playground for one of Manhattan's wealthiest families. And Logan had driven all the way up from his Connecticut home to take full advantage of that new function.

Following a semicircular drive directly before the building, he parked the car, stepped out, ascended the steps—worn and incredibly wide—and walked past the lines of white-painted Adirondack chairs into the lobby. It was warm and welcoming, indirectly lit, with a mellow, golden, faintly hazy atmosphere redolent of wood smoke. He felt the oddly pleasing sensation of a fly sinking into amber.

A reception desk of cinnamon-colored wood, glowing from what appeared to be the application of fifty coats of lacquer, stood directly ahead. A middle-aged woman behind it looked up at his approach, smiled.

"I'm Jeremy Logan," he told her. "Checking in."

"Just a minute." The woman consulted a tablet computer tucked behind the desk as if it were an anachronism to be kept hidden. "Ah, yes. Dr. Logan. You'll be joining us for six weeks."

"That's right."

"Very good." She studied the tablet for a few more moments. "Dr. *Jeremy* Logan?" She looked up suddenly, recognition flashing in her eyes before being quickly suppressed. "But it says here 'historian.'"

"I am an historian. Among other things."

After a moment, the woman nodded, then glanced back down at the tablet. "I see you've been booked into the Thomas Cole cabin. By Mr. Hartshorn himself. That cabin is usually reserved for musicians or artists—writers are always assigned rooms in the main lodge."

"I'll remember to thank him."

"It's just past the boathouse, not two minutes' walk. I could show it to you now, and then you can park your car in the assigned lot and retrieve your bags."

"Thank you, I'd appreciate that."

Turning around and unlocking a wooden cabinet behind her, she took a large key from one of several dozen brass pegs. Then, relocking the cabinet and coming out from behind the desk, she smiled once again, then led the way back outside and down the hard-packed dirt road to a nearby path into the woods, flanked by walkway lights in Tiffany-style glass. The perfume of pine was almost overpowering. Every fifty feet or so a smaller path diverged from the main one, heading either to the left or the right, each with a small carved signpost: ALBERT BIERSTADT, THOMAS MORAN, WILLIAM HART.

In short order, she turned down a final bend in the path, where the signboard read Thomas Cole. Just ahead, half hidden among the trees, was a two-story Mission-style cabin, charmingly rusticated and yet of obviously modern construction, with a peeled-log facade and granite fieldstone foundation.

The woman handed him the key. "I'm sure you'll find everything you need inside," she said. She looked at her watch. "It's almost eight. The kitchen closes at nine, so you'll probably want to get settled in without delay."

"Thank you," Logan said. She smiled once again, then turned and retreated back down the pathway.

Hefting the key, Logan mounted the steps, then unlocked the front door and stepped in. Snapping on the bank of lights just within, he quickly took in the surroundings: wide-planked floorboards, antique rugs, a modern worktable with a Herman Miller Aeron chair set before it, built-in bookcases and cabinets of mahogany, a huge fireplace of rough stone, and a freestanding spiral staircase going up to a bedroom/sleeping loft above. Through a door in the far wall of the room, he could see a kitchen complete with microwave, Wolf stovetop, and refrigerated wine cellar. It was an aesthetically pleasing, yet highly functional, combination of old and new.

As he looked around, Logan allowed himself a slow, contented sigh. "Kit," he told his wife, "I think this place is exactly right. And I've given myself six weeks. If I can't finish it here, then I guess it may never get finished."

Then, leaving the lights on, he exited the cabin to retrieve his luggage.

3

Twenty minutes later, Logan exited the cabin and went back down the path, the little guide lights illuminating the way like fairy lanterns in a forest. Coming out onto the wide central lawn, he approached the main building, then stopped once again to admire it. The sense of optimism that had come over him as he'd surveyed the cabin had not left.

Cloudwater called itself an "artists' colony." Situated in the heart of Adirondack State Park, it was tenanted at any one time by several dozen artists, writers, and researchers who came for one- to two-month stays in order to work on their individual projects: whether it be a painting, a novel, or a concerto. Each of the artists-in-residence had his or her private room in the vast lodge or—in the case of musicians and artists—the separate, secluded cottages scattered among the heavily wooded grounds. It was not a vacation spot—people who came here, came here to work, and rules were imposed to make sure things stayed that way. There was no cocktail hour, no structured activities save the occasional after-dinner lecture and the art movies shown on Saturday evenings. Visitors to an individual's cottage were by invitation only. Lunches were private, served in one's room or cabin, while breakfast and dinner were served in the lodge.

Climbing the steps and entering the building, Logan noticed a few people, in groups of two or three, walking through the soaring lobby, speaking among themselves in quiet tones. The ceiling was supported by pairs of huge curved beams, rising toward each other from opposite sides of the room, so that Logan felt almost as if he were inside the ribs of an inverted ship. Between these beams, and acting as crown molding, was a decorative, antlerlike fretwork of remarkable intricacy. Heads of bear, deer, and moose, apparently many decades old, were mounted on the walls, interspersed with prize fish on plaques, old photographs of the park, and paintings of the Hudson River School.

Stopping one group and inquiring as to the location of the dining room, Logan thanked them and was moving on when a voice sounded behind him. "Dr. Logan?"

He turned to see a tall, rather heavyset man in his early seventies, with a florid face and an almost leonine mane of snowy white hair. He smiled and extended one hand. "I'm Greg Hartshorn."

Logan shook the hand. "Pleased to meet you."

Logan had, of course, heard of Gregory Hartshorn. He'd been a prominent painter of the Lyrical Abstraction school who had founded a gallery in mid-1960s New York, where he made a fortune selling his and others' paintings. He had put art aside about thirty years later in order to take on the position of Cloudwater's resident director.

"I was just heading in to dinner," Logan said.

"I hope you'll find it excellent. Before you do, could I have a minute of your time?" And without waiting for an answer, Hartshorn steered Logan across the lobby and through an unmarked door into a cozy office, its walls crowded with sketches, watercolors, woodblock prints—but, Logan noticed, not a single one of Hartshorn's own works.

"Make yourself comfortable," Hartshorn said, gesturing Logan to a seat on a sofa before a desk crowded with paperwork.

"Have you given it up entirely?" Logan asked, indicating the art-covered walls.

Hartshorn chuckled. "I still do the odd study now and then. But they never seem to mature into finished works. It's remarkable, really, how much administrative work there is to do at a place like Cloudwater."

Logan nodded. He had an idea why Hartshorn had asked to speak to him, but he'd let the resident director bring it up himself.

Hartshorn took a seat behind the desk, interlaced his fingers on the scarred wooden surface, then leaned forward. "I'll be brief, Jeremy—may I call you Jeremy?"

"Please."

"I know your CV states you're a professor of history at Yale. I also know you registered here as an historian. But . . . well, in recent years it seems you've become very well known for a more, shall we say, sensational line of work."

Logan remained silent.

"I just—without prying, you understand—was curious how you planned to spend your time here at Cloudwater."

"You mean, am I going to be involved in anything sensational?"

Hartshorn laughed a little self-consciously. "To be blunt, yes. As you know, for all its rustic charm, Cloudwater is devoted to creative work. Whether they are given grants or pay large sums of money, people come here specifically to pursue their muse in as undisturbed a fashion as possible. I like to think of time spent here as a kind of luxuriant monasticism."

Logan had been planning to thank the resident director for assigning him the Thomas Cole cabin. Now, however, he realized this had not been done out of munificence—it had been to isolate him from the bulk of Cloudwater's residents.

"If you're wondering whether zombies are going to start walking the grounds, or spectral chains will rattle loudly in the night, you have nothing to fear," he replied.

"That's a relief. But I admit to being rather more concerned about camera crews and journalists."

"If they come, it won't be for me," Logan said. "I'm here in precisely the capacity I stated on my application. For years, I've been trying to complete a monograph on heresy in the Middle Ages. Work, and various side projects, keep forestalling that. I'm hoping the peace and quiet of Cloudwater will provide the concentration I need, allow me to put the finishing touches on the paper."

Hartshorn's interlaced fingers seemed to relax slightly. "Thank you for being candid. Frankly, your application for a residence here became a matter of discussion for the board of directors. I spoke in your favor. I'm glad to hear I won't regret doing so."

Logan nodded.

"But surely you'll understand my apprehension. For example, do you know a Randall Jessup?"

"Randall Jessup?" Logan frowned. "I went to Yale with somebody by that name."

"Well, he's a lieutenant ranger in New York's Division of Forest Protection now. And he came by here earlier today, asking when you were expected."

"How could he know I was coming to Cloudwater? I haven't spoken with him in years."

"And therein lies my concern. I don't know how he got wind of it. But your visiting Cloudwater comes under the heading of local news. For all its size, the Adirondacks can sometimes feel like a small community. Somebody on our staff must have recognized your name, and told somebody else, who then told somebody else. . . . You know how these things spread."

Logan knew.

"But in any case, let's say no more on the subject. I'm assured you've come here as a scholar and a historian—and I wish you the best of luck finishing your monograph. If there's anything I can do to make your stay more comfortable, please let me know. And now, I won't detain you any longer. The kitchen's closing shortly."

And with that, Hartshorn stood up and offered his hand once again.

4

The dining room was about what Logan had expected of an erst-while Adirondack "Great Camp": full of Mission-style furniture, Japanese screens, chandeliers of woven birch wood, display cases stuffed with geodes and Native American artifacts, and a cut-stone fireplace large enough to roast a horse in. It somehow man-aged to be both rustic and opulent at the same time. Mindful of what Hartshorn had told him, Logan chose an inconspicuous table in a far corner, receiving only a few curious stares. The food proved to be excellent—braised short ribs and pickled ramps that he paired with a sublime Châteauneuf-du-Pape—although due to the late hour the service was a trifle rushed, and it was a few minutes before ten when he made his way back out into the lobby and onto the broad, rambling front porch. He stopped there a moment, admiring the dome of stars overhead, the lake murmuring and lapping at the far end of the grand swath of lawn.

As he did so, someone sitting in one of the chairs that lined the porch stirred. "Jeremy?"

Logan turned toward the sound as the figure stood up and approached, a worn leather satchel in one hand. As the figure came into the light, Logan felt a slightly delayed shock of recognition. "Randall!"

The man smiled and shook Logan's hand. "Glad you can still recognize me."

"You've hardly changed." And it was true—although Logan hadn't seen his friend in two decades, Randall Jessup didn't look all that much different than he had during his undergraduate days at Yale. The sandy brown hair was a little thinner, perhaps, and the tanned face and crow's feet at the corners of his eyes spoke of a life lived mostly outdoors, but there was still an almost palpable sense of youth emanating from the tall, slight man with the perpetual expression of thoughtful concern.

"They told me you were here, but they wouldn't tell me where you were staying," Jessup said. He was dressed in the olive shirt and pants and sand-colored, trooper-style hat of a forest ranger, and he wore a heavy service belt with a holster. "Just that you were in one of the cabins. Security here is like Camp David."

"It's not far. Follow me—we can catch up inside."

Logan led the way across the lawn, then down the path to his cottage. He opened the door, waved Jessup in with one hand.

"Nice place," Jessup said, looking around as Logan turned on a light just within.

Luxuriant monasticism, Logan thought. "I haven't unpacked yet, so I have no idea where anything is. I had the foresight to bring along a bottle of vodka, though. Share a glass with me?"

"Love one," Jessup said as he let his satchel slide to the floor.

Logan dug the bottle of Belvedere out of his small pile of luggage at the base of the stairs, took it into the kitchen, searched the cupboards for a minute until he found a couple of cut-glass tumblers, then filled them with handfuls of ice from the freezer and poured a few fingers of vodka into each. Carrying them back out of the kitchen, he handed one to Jessup, cracked open a window, and they sat down on a leather couch that wrapped around one corner of the room. A standing lamp with a shade made of painted birch bark stood at one end, and Logan pulled its chain, casting a pool of tawny light across the corner of the room.

As they sipped their drinks, Logan thought back over his memories of Jessup. They had been fairly close their junior year at Yale, when Logan had been a history major and Jessup was studying philosophy—and taking himself, as often happens with budding philosophers, rather seriously. That year, he'd discovered a particular school of writers—Thoreau, Emerson, Octavius Brooks Frothingham—and became deeply interested in transcendentalism. He spent a part of his senior year off campus on an unusual program in the Yukon. When he'd gone on to Yale's School of Forestry and Environmental Studies, the two had lost touch.

"Tell me about yourself," Logan said. "Are you married?"

"Yes. I've got two kids, Franklin, twelve, and Hannah, nine."

Logan smiled inwardly. Even the children were named after philosophers.

"How about you?" Jessup asked.

"I was."

"Divorced?"

Logan shook his head. "She died several years ago."

"Oh. God. I'm sorry."

"It's all right." Logan nodded at his friend's uniform. "I should have guessed you'd end up a ranger. Far from the madding crowd and all that. Did you join right out of Yale?"

"No." Jessup removed his hat, placed it on the sofa between them. "I bummed around the world for a year or two—India, Tibet, Burma, Brazil, Nepal. Hiked through a lot of forests, climbed a lot of mountains. Did a lot of reading, did a lot of thinking. Then I came home. I grew up about fifty miles from here, you know, in Plattsburgh. I knew the Adirondacks pretty well from half a dozen summers spent at camp on Tupper Lake. So I joined the forest rangers." He gave a funny, self-deprecating smile.

"And you've risen to lieutenant, or so I hear."

Jessup laughed. "Sounds more important than it is. Actually, I'm about halfway up the totem pole. Technically, I'm supervisor for Zone Five-A of Region Five. I've got six rangers reporting to me." He paused. "I can guess what you're thinking. I should have been a captain by now. I mean, it's been over fifteen years. Oh, I've had the opportunity. But I just don't want to sit behind a desk. We live outside Saranac Lake, part of my jurisdiction. Built the place myself. You don't need a lot of money to live well here, and Suzanne and the kids are happy."

Logan nodded. Sounded like the self-reliant, self-directed Jessup he remembered.

He knew his old friend had something on his mind—the fact that he'd come by twice today to see him said as much. Logan had a gift for empathy—he had an instinct that, when he chose to use it, let him sense, to a greater or lesser degree, the emotions and thoughts of the person he was with. But he chose not to employ it now; Jessup would, he knew, get around to it when he was ready.

Instead, he took another sip of his drink. "How did we ever become friends, anyway? I don't recall."

"We were rivals before we were friends. Anne Brannigan—remember her?"

"No. Yes. She had a moon and star stitched on her backpack and was a vegan even before the term was invented."

Jessup laughed again. "That's right." He sipped his drink. "So you stayed at Yale."

"Got my doctorate at Magdalen College, Oxford. Spent a few years of my own wandering the world, but not places as exotic as Nepal or Burma—mostly old libraries, monasteries, and the churches of England and the Continent. Then I came back to teach a colloquium on the Black Death when the Yale professor who'd been planning to give it fell ill." He shrugged. "Never left."

"That's not what I've heard," Jessup said, in a quiet voice.

"You're referring to my, ah, avocation."

Jessup nodded.

"The strange one. The one that tends to get my picture in the papers now and then."

Jessup nodded again. "You were doing that even back at Yale. I remember our senior year, when you proved how that ghost that supposedly haunted Saybrook was just a secret tradition, handed down from one graduating student and entrusted to another." He paused. "I read that profile of you in *People* a year or two ago."

"Terrible photo. Made me look fat."

"And you call yourself an . . . ?"

"Enigmalogist. Somebody else came up with the term, actually, but it seems to have stuck."

"I remember how the article described it. It said you study phenomena beyond the bounds of regular science: investigate the strange and inexplicable, prove things most people would label occult or supernatural."

"Or disprove them—as with the Saybrook ghost."

"Right." Jessup hesitated a moment, seemed to come to some kind of decision. "Look, Jeremy—you've probably guessed my stopping by isn't just to renew an old acquaintance."

"Although it's nice to see you again, the thought had occurred to me."

"Well, do you mind if I share something with you? Between ourselves—for the time being, anyway."

"Of course."

Jessup shook the ice in his empty glass. "Can I get a dividend first?"

"How remiss of me." Taking the glass into the kitchen, Logan splashed some more vodka into it and gave it back to Jessup. The ranger took a sip, paused a moment, looked around the room, and then—after taking a deep breath—started to talk.

5

"Over the last three months," Jessup began, "two hikers—backpackers—have been killed not far from here."

Logan waited, listening.

"There are a lot of similarities between the two killings. Both men were young and extremely fit, knowledgeable about forestry issues and the park. And they were both members of the Adirondack 'Forty-Sixers.'"

Logan nodded his understanding. This was the group whose membership was limited to those who had climbed all forty-six Adirondack peaks over four thousand feet. The requirements included both mountains with blazed trails and the trailless peaks, and, as he recalled, at least one winter ascent. He and Kit had once, years back, entertained hopes of joining the elite club—before reality intervened.

"Both were savagely mauled to death," Jessup went on. "Both were killed in roughly the same remote location—and both, as it happens, during a full moon."

"What remote location, exactly?"

"West of the Five Ponds Wilderness." Jessup paused a moment, and night sounds from the open window—the rustle of leaves picked up by a stray gust of wind, the hoot of an owl—filled the silence.

"These hard-core backpackers are a breed apart," Jessup said. "No achievement, no matter how hard-won, is ever enough. So once they've bagged all forty-six peaks, some of them go on to score other bragging rights. Three mountains seem to be favorite." He pulled a leatherbound journal from a breast pocket, leafed through it, studied a page for a moment. "Avalanche Mountain, number sixty-three—close to higher and more famous mountains and an obvious choice. North River Mountain, number fifty-six, just shy of four thousand feet and coveted because the official state surveyor, Ebenezer Emmons, climbed it immediately before his famous 1836 ascent of Whiteface Mountain. But the most coveted prize is Desolation Mountain. At only thirty-two hundred feet, it's not even in the top hundred." He replaced the journal. "But its claim to fame, and what makes it such an attractive target, is its remoteness. The Desolation Lake area is probably the wildest and most isolated section of the entire park—even more so than the Silver Lake Wilderness or Wilcox Lake. Not only that, but the terrain there is terrible for hiking—no access roads and few motorized lakes, covered with blowdowns, outwash bogs, all sorts of other hazardous conditions. Unless you know what you're doing, and you're incredibly motivated, it's almost impossible to reach. The climb itself is the easy part." He laughed almost bitterly, shook his head. "That's why it's known among the ADK climbing elite as 'heartbreak forty-seven.'"

As quickly as it came, the laugh died in Jessup's throat. "Both hikers were found in the vicinity of the mountain. As you can imagine, there's not a lot of traffic through there, and by the time the bodies were discovered each was in an advanced state of decomposition. As a result, the autopsies were somewhat inconclusive, but given the violence inflicted on the corpses, the verdict in both was mauling by a rogue bear."

Jessup took another sip of his drink. "We've tried to keep details of the story quiet—places like Cloudwater here, for example, need that kind of publicity like they need a hole in the head. But rumors spread, and the locals all know."

"I'm sorry to hear about it," Logan said. "But why the urgency to tell me?"

Again, Jessup hesitated. "I told you the official conclusion of the autopsy. But the fact is, a few of us rangers aren't so certain. Black bears—the only kind found in the park—aren't numerous, nor are they known to be vicious. A single death by mauling is very rare, but two . . ." His voice trailed off.

"There's a long history of wild animals turning aggressive toward man," Logan said. "Look at the Tsavo lions."

"I know. And that's what I've been telling myself. But you have to remember, I spent a lot of summers here growing up. I heard my share of the local rumors and fables. Most visitors here stick to the tamer locales like Lake Placid. Domesticated, populous. They don't know there are millions of acres out here—not that far of a drive, either—that aren't like that. Some places to this day have never seen a man's footprint, or echoed with the chop of an ax."

"Spoken like a true philosopher," Logan said gently, trying to lighten the atmosphere. Jessup grinned a little abashedly. "I suppose you've sent search parties through the area where the bodies were found, looking for the animal?"

"A brief one. It yielded nothing."

"Anyway, it sounds like you aren't satisfied with the official story."

"I'm not sure I'd ever admit to that," Jessup said quickly.

"But you think there might be more to the story. That something else might be going on."

"You know what Emerson said. 'Nature and books belong to the eyes that see them.'"

"I knew you'd get around to Emerson eventually. But why bring it to me? I'm no Natty Bumppo. The last trail I set foot on was Newport's Cliff Walk, which doesn't even count."

"It's not that kind of skill I'm looking for. I can't say why exactly, but the peculiar circumstances of these deaths . . . something feels wrong to me. And I say that as someone who has policed these forests for many years. But I'm too close to this—both as a ranger, and as a resident. I need someone with your objectivity . . . and your, um, unusual skill set."

So that's it. Logan felt dismay settling over him. Although he'd never admit it to his old friend, this was the last complication he needed right now. It was going to be hard enough just summoning the intellectual energy to finish his monograph—what more if he had to traipse around the vast park on a nebulous errand he wasn't qualified for?

"Look, Randall, I can understand your concern," he said. "If I was in your position, I'd feel the same way—"

"It's not that," Jessup said, a faint hint of stubbornness creeping into his tone. "I don't feel responsible for these deaths—there are many areas of the park so remote we don't even try to patrol them. I just feel that if I asked you to take a brief look into these deaths . . . well, then I'd have done my due diligence. And I'd sleep better at night, knowing that."

"You say something feels wrong. What, exactly?"

"I don't know. If I knew, I wouldn't be asking you for counsel. But I just can't seem to shake the premonition that something bad is going to happen again . . . and soon."

"I'd like to help," Logan said. "But I don't see what expertise I can offer. I'm no pathologist. I'm no backwoodsman. And the fact is I came up here to finish a paper I've been working on for almost two years—"

"Just go to Pike Hollow," Jessup interrupted. "As a personal favor to me. It's the town nearest the sites of the killings. Go there tomorrow, ask around—under the radar, of course—and then have dinner with me. Meet my wife and kids. And then, if you don't want to take it further, I'll let the whole thing drop."

"I . . ." Logan began, then stopped. There was no mistaking his friend's concern. And it seemed pointless to protest anymore. He took a deep breath. "Okay. But your wife had better be a good cook."

Jessup smiled again—this time with obvious relief. "I don't think you'll have cause to complain." He picked up the leather satchel, pulled out two thick manila folders, passed them over to Logan. "Here are copies of the case files. Look them over when you get the chance. But keep it to yourself. The park is a crazy quilt of overlapping jurisdictions. Since so many of the smaller communities have no police departments of their own, the state police often take the leading role in serious crimes such as rape or murder—not that those are common. It's true I'm a Department of Conservation officer, authorized to enforce all state rules and regulations, but I'm not really at liberty to bring a layman into the investigation."

"Great. You want me to investigate, but you don't."

"I'm sure this isn't the first job you've taken requiring discretion. I understand your SSBI clearance has an open exit date."

"I haven't taken the job, remember? But you're right. Give me your address, let me know what time dinner is tomorrow, and I'll see you there."

Jessup pulled out the small, worn journal again, scrawled quickly on a page, tore it off, and handed it to Logan. "Seven o'clock work for you?"

When Logan nodded, Jessup stood. "Then I'll let you get settled in. Thank you, Jeremy. I know this is an imposition. But I wouldn't ask if I didn't think it was important." His gaze drifted toward the case files.

"Get on home. I'll see you tomorrow."

Jessup seemed about to say something else. But then he simply nodded, picked up the empty satchel, shook Logan's hand, seated his ranger's hat squarely on his head, and stepped out of the cabin into the night.

6

The next morning, Logan had an early breakfast in the big lodge, then got into his car and left Cloudwater. He now regretted promising Jessup he'd look into the murders; in the chill light of day he was even more convinced there was nothing he could add to the official investigation, and his laptop, books, and notes—placed on the living room worktable of his cabin—silently chastised him for not getting immediately to work. But he was to have dinner with the Jessup family that evening; it seemed best to make a cursory effort—Randall had asked him as a personal favor, after all—which would then allow him to report no success and get on with what he'd come here to finish.

And so he pointed the nose of his car westward, following Route 3 as it threaded its way between the steep flanks of rising mountains and along the shores of rushing streams. It occurred to him as he drove that he had never penetrated this deeply into the park before. It was a forty-mile drive to the hamlet of Pike Hollow, and the farther he went, the more the things he was accustomed to seeing began to fall away. First went the summer camps with the fake Indian names and wooden signboards, invariably situated on the shores of lakes. Next went such tourist attractions as the curio shops offering lynx tails and arrowheads and other backwoods bric-a-brac. Then, even the establishments that catered to the locals began to vanish: gas stations; ATV and snowmobile repair shops; turnouts for private logging roads. Past Sevey he left Route 3 for 3A, a narrow road that plunged still farther westward, into a pine forest so deep the overhanging branches formed a kind of woven tunnel, beneath which a perpetual evening reigned. The air became increasingly humid and moist. This road was in far worse repair, its blacktop so cracked and heaved that sections of it could barely be called paved. Passing cars were infrequent. As the reception bars on his cell phone disappeared one by one, Logan became aware of a vague sense of apprehension: if anything should happen to his Lotus Elan S4, he doubted that there was a mechanic within a hundred miles capable of repairing, let alone finding parts for, the fifty-year-old sports car.

But there was another component to his growing feeling of apprehension—the forest itself. It gave the impression of being almost immeasurably old; he felt that he could pull onto the shoulder at any point, walk off into the trees, and within minutes—if he wasn't already lost—be where no human being had set foot before. The growing lack of human habitation was somehow unsettling. Logan felt almost like an intruder here: a tiny, insignificant intruder, to be tolerated perhaps but given no comfort or assistance. He recalled the lines of an old English ghost story, set in a remote Canadian wilderness: *The bleak splendours of these remote and lonely forests overwhelmed him with the sense of his own littleness. That stern quality of the tangled backwood which can only be described as merciless and terrible, rose out of these far blue woods swimming upon the horizon, and revealed itself. He understood the silent warning. He realized his own utter helplessness.*

A sudden bend in the road, and Pike Hollow was upon him: a one-street town leading north off 3A, home to eight hundred inhabitants according to the faded road sign, surrounded on all sides by dark, rising forest as if built into the bowl of an inverted snow globe. Here, at least, there was a small degree of civilization: shops, houses, a diner, their facades all pushed up close against the road as if grasping at a life preserver. His roadster received the occasional curious look as he drove slowly through town. This was no tourist destination, as the decrepitude of many buildings and the obvious lack of affluence made clear. Here and there, narrow lanes led off the main street, inevitably ending in a huddle of sad-looking residences hard up against the encircling forest. He glanced over his shoulder, past the buildings toward the south, to the unbroken wall of trees. A few miles away, he knew, lay the Five Ponds Wilderness. And beyond that, Desolation Lake—and the site of the two murders.

He made a circuit of the town—an undertaking that took up less than ten minutes—and then pulled over to a spot near where he'd first entered and killed the engine, considering how best to proceed. This was a task he'd done many times before—entering an unfamiliar town with the intent of prizing information out of locals who might or might not be eager to talk—and he had developed a number of roles through which to accomplish it. He considered, then rejected, posing as a tourist—a tourist wouldn't ask the kind of questions he was going to. He also rejected impersonating a potential real estate buyer: it didn't seem particularly credible, and besides, people would be unlikely to talk about unpleasant subjects to someone who might bring money into the town. In the end he settled on the guise of nature photographer. This not only gave him a believable motive for being so far off the beaten track, but it gave him reason to ask a lot of questions under the pretense of seeking colorful locations to shoot. And a photographer wouldn't likely be scared off by rumors of evil deeds: in fact, they might arouse his professional curiosity.

He reached into the glove compartment, pulled out a pair of heavy tortoiseshell glasses, and put them on, just on the off chance he might be recognized. Then, getting out of the car, he opened the boot and rummaged among various disguises and props, at last pulling out a suitably faded photographer's vest and a Nikon SLR with a telephoto lens: the camera wasn't in working order, but since it was only for effect it had been much cheaper to purchase that way. He shrugged into the vest, slipped the camera strap over one shoulder, and prepared to make his way down the main street.

Pike Hollow had no police force of its own, so Logan had to content himself with speaking to a variety of shop owners. He dropped in first at a barber, where—although he didn't need one—he got a haircut from a fellow named Sam, who, it seemed, lived only to catch fish with a fly rod on the Ausable River. Next, he visited the town's sole restaurant, where he had an early lunch, served by a talkative waitress. This was followed by a stop at a dry goods store, where after a lengthy conversation with the proprietor he purchased a pair of socks that he could at least justify to himself, since (the merchant told him) a cold snap was in the forecast.

Each stop provided him with additional information, which he was then able to leverage in future stops to gain still more information. While the townspeople were obviously concerned about the recent backpacker deaths, they did not seem to be particularly shy about discussing them. And the more he learned about the town and the area, and the more he could pass himself off as a knowledgeable visitor, the more people seemed to open up. After each stop, he took out a notebook, made entries on what he had learned, and cross-correlated any common threads.

One thread in particular seemed to crop up in every conversation.

Finally, around half past three, he walked into Fred's Hideaway, a bar at the far end of town. It was, as he'd hoped, empty save for Fred. Logan ordered a beer, surmising it was the beverage he could nurse the longest while engaging the bartender in conversation. All beers were bottled—there was nothing on tap—nor were there any imported brands. Logan chose a Michelob Light.

After the initial pleasantries were complete, Logan was quick to establish himself—with a variety of observations he'd picked up during his previous conversations—as someone who had at least a passing familiarity with the region and its news. As they spoke, Fred nodded with a pretense of sagacity, every so often stopping to pluck a bar towel off his left shoulder and wipe the worn varnish with it.

"I'm a freelance photographer," Logan said in response to a question from Fred. "Don't work for any particular magazine or bureau. Nobody sends me anywhere, or hands me assignments. That means it's up to me to find the most interesting pictures I can."

He took a pull from his beer as Fred gave another sagacious nod.

"So I was thinking maybe I could get some shots of the region where these terrible accidents took place," Logan went on. "You know, the killings of those backpackers."

"The Wilderness?" Fred asked, disbelief creeping into his voice.

"Yes, that's it. The Five Ponds Wilderness. It's pretty close, right?"

"Couldn't get in there. Least not without a helicopter, or maybe a tank. That's bad country in there. Nobody goes in except the occasional crazy hiker. And the last two hikers that went in there didn't come out again." Fred put a knowing fingertip to the side of his nose.

"No guides?"

Fred shook his head. "You'd be awful hard-pressed to find one—especially after what's happened."

"Well, maybe I can just go to, you know, the edge of it. What I'm really looking for is a shot of a bear." And here Logan leaned in a little conspiratorially. "I mean, if I sold *that* picture—the killer bear that mauled two backpackers—who's going to dispute whether I snapped the right bear or not?"

"Wasn't no bear as killed those youngsters," Fred said, leaning in a little himself.

Logan feigned surprise. "No bear?"

"Nope."

"What killed them, then?"

Fred hesitated. "Don't know as I should say, rightly. Haven't got any proof. That is, unless you call sixty years of hearing tales, and seeing things with my own eyes, proof."

Fred was just about the most garrulous of the Pike Hollow residents Logan had spoken with. He also seemed to know more than most. Yet on this one particularly important point he seemed reticent. Logan realized he would have to show his hand just a little. He drained his beer, ordered another, and invited Fred to have one, on him. When it came, he said: "You must be talking about that clan."

At this, Fred nodded. "The Blakeneys," he said, popping the cap off a bottle of Budweiser and placing it on the bar in front of him.

This was a darkly hinted nugget that, in one form or another, Logan had picked up from just about everyone he'd talked to: the town's deep, aiding, and long-standing mistrust of the so-called Blakeney clan.

"Tell me about these Blakeneys," Logan asked offhandedly. "Everything I've heard is just rumor."

Fred hesitated again.

"I won't say I heard it from you."

Fred considered a moment, then shrugged. "Guess there's nothing wrong with saying what everyone in town knows already. Those Blakeneys have lived in the area since before anyone could remember."

"Where, exactly?"

Fred pointed southwest, over Logan's shoulder. "They've got a big, rambling old stead on the edge of the Wilderness."

"What's it like?"

Fred shrugged. "They don't care for outsiders, and that's a fact. Fenced themselves in, keep to themselves, make a living off the land, rarely set foot in town. Don't know anybody who's been inside, but from what I hear they've got all sorts of ramshackle buildings and things in there."

Logan pushed his beer bottle to one side, untouched. "Sounds strange, all right. But why would people think they had anything to do with the murders?"

"First, there ain't many bears around these parts. You find them in the High Peaks region now and again, but they avoid humans. Second, I've been hearing strange stories about those Blakeneys ever since I was a kid—stories that make me think them capable of murder . . . and more."

"What kind of strange stories?"

Fred took a pull from his beer. "They've lived deep in the woods for too long. People do that, you know, and it *changes* them. But from what I hear tell, that clan was always vicious. That, and . . . well, there was a rash of missing children around here back in the seventies—oh, it got hushed up, but everybody knows who took 'em—and why."

Fred was voluble now, but even so Logan didn't want to ask *why* aloud. He merely raised his eyebrows inquiringly.

"Rituals. Dark rituals. And I don't mean black magic—I mean something worse. The way those Blakeneys have dealings with the animals of the deep forest—well, it's unnatural, people say. Communing with nature that way, becoming part of it. The wrong part. Who knows what's become of them, or what they do, back up in there?"

"That's disturbing. But why would they want to kill those backpackers?"

Even though the bar was empty, Fred leaned in still farther. "Mister, I can tell you that in just two words: *tainted blood*."

7

Back in his car, Logan took a moment to jot down notes from his conversation with Fred the bartender, then he went back and looked over what he'd written earlier in the day. All the people he'd spoken to in Pike Hollow agreed on two things: one, a bear hadn't mauled the backpackers, and two, the Blakeney clan was mixed up in it. Exactly how, they could not or would not say.

His final stop of the day, then, seemed an obvious one.

He started up the engine, then drove slowly down Main Street to its intersection with 3A. When he'd asked more precise directions to the Blakeney compound, Fred—after numerous warnings against an attempted visit and dire predictions about what might happen if he pursued one—finally relented. "Head west maybe a mile and you'll see a turnoff on the left," he'd said. "Ain't hardly visible, no markings or signs or nothing. Only way to tell is it's the only dirt track you'll come across along that stretch of highway."

He pulled back onto 3A, watching the odometer as he went. It was only quarter past four, but under the heavy, sky-obscuring canopy of the surrounding forest it seemed much later. At a little more than a mile past the Pike Hollow intersection, he came across what he assumed had to be the road into the Blakeney compound: little more than a narrow cut in the otherwise unbroken mass of foliage, a muddy, deeply rutted dirt path that twisted sharply away, vanishing from sight. As Fred the bartender had told him, it wasn't hardly visible.

Nosing his Lotus into the turnoff, he began making his bone-jarring way down the lane. It was so narrow that branches brushed and scraped against both sides of the small vehicle. After creeping ahead about a quarter of a mile, he stopped: he'd bottomed out the suspension twice already in the deep ruts and didn't dare go any farther. There was no room to turn around, and no room to pass an oncoming vehicle: he'd simply have to leave the car where it was.

He tried opening the driver's door, but the living wall of undergrowth that hemmed in the car made it physically impossible. In the end, he was forced to put the top halfway down and crawl out over the windscreen and hood. He paused a moment in the lane to gather his wits and reconnoiter, allowing his preternaturally heightened senses free rein.

In this path that was little more than a man-made tube bored through the woods, it was even more humid than it had been on the road. The heavy fir branches around and above sweated a cold dew, and chill vapors wafted up from the ground. He glanced back at the roadster, plugging the dirt road like a cork plugged the neck of a bottle. Once more Logan felt, even more strongly, the sense of being an intruder here—for two reasons now rather than just one.

As he began making his way down the path, following its capricious twistings through ever-denser forest, he became aware of something else. All day—as he'd made the drive to Pike Hollow, as he'd toured the town—he had heard birdsong. But here, all was quiet. He had the strong impression that the woods were listening. It was all he could do not to tiptoe forward.

A final bend in the path, and it suddenly widened before him into a small clearing, the ends of the branches and brush on both sides hacked sharply off and gathered into rude, decaying piles. A blade of a machete with an ancient, hand-carved handle was buried deep in the trunk of a nearby red maple. But it was not this that caught Logan's attention, or what made him stop abruptly in something close to disbelief.

Directly ahead, the rutted path ended in a wall: a wall at least eight feet high, constructed of innumerable twigs of similar size and length, arranged vertically, pressed tightly together and lashed with brown, rusting baling wire. There was no obvious break in the wall to indicate where it might open—if indeed it did open. The twigs had been fitted together with fantastic, obsessive precision, like some kind of rustic, diabolical jigsaw puzzle. While individually the twigs were relatively thin, there were so many of them, and they appeared to extend to such a depth—at least a foot or more—that the wall seemed impenetrable. It was clearly very old, and something about it—the texture of the twigs, or the fantastically, compulsively complex architecture by which they had been joined—unnerved Logan. His senses told him there was an otherness here; something that was not right. Fred the bartender had spoken about how the clan communed with nature, but what Logan felt very strongly—almost like a warning cry in his head—was something deeply *un*natural.

He walked along the disquieting, makeshift wall, following it first to the left, then turning and following it to the right, to the points where it vanished into the forest. The trees and undergrowth were so thick at both points that it was impossible to follow its circumference past the opening offered by the clearing, but it seemed obvious the wall encircled a large area, at least a few acres and perhaps more.

Logan opened his mouth to call out through the thick barricade, only to find that his voice had left him. He swallowed, licked his lips, tried again. "Hello," he called, in little more than a croak. He cleared his throat. "Hello!" he said more loudly. "My name is Logan. I wonder if I could talk to you for just a minute."

Nothing. The compound beyond the fortification of twigs and baling wire was as silent as the surrounding forest.

Now Logan stepped back to look past and over the wall. Beyond it and to the right a mountain rose steeply, fringed heavily in dense pines. The upper section of a single structure was visible on its flanks, over the top of the wall: a very large, gambrel-roofed building, covered in rude, lichen-covered shingles. At this distance, it appeared to be in an advanced state of decay. He could see two ranks of windows, huddled together under the broadly hipped roof. Candles glimmered in the lower of the two ranks, their lights distorted by ancient panes of glass. The upper windows were shuttered and dark. Whatever other structures lay within, they were evidently on lower ground, hidden by the bizarre wall of fitted twigs.

It was growing even darker under the forest canopy; soon it would be too dark to see. Logan approached the fortification again, moving slowly along it, trying to find an aperture through which he could see what lay beyond. Suddenly he found one: it was near the center of the clearing, and had obviously been made intentionally—this was clear by the careful way the twigs surrounding it had been whittled away. The hole was at eye level and cone shaped, wider on the inside than it was on the outside. As Logan looked through it—making out in the briefest of glimpses a number of decrepit outbuildings, a barn of the most ancient appearance imaginable, a fenced area for crops, and what appeared to be a large refuse pile to one side—he realized that it must have been made for the residents to look out.

Even as he stared, his empathetic instincts told him, once again, something on the far side of that enclosure was strange—very strange.

At that same moment, the aperture was abruptly filled with the barrel of a gun, large-bored and rusted. "You git away now," came a harsh, deep voice from the far side of the wall.

Logan swallowed. "I don't mean to trespass," he said. "I just wanted to know if I could ask you a few—"

He went silent at the sound of a shell being ratcheted into the chamber. "Git off our land," the uncouth voice said. "Or the last thing you'll be seeing on this earth is the muzzle of this here goddamn shotgun."

Logan needed no further persuasion. Without another word, he backed out of the clearing and down the rutted, muddy path. Then he turned around, walked quickly to his car, scrambled in over the hood, and made his way in reverse down the hellish, branch-choked lane and onto the safety of State Route 3A.

8

Logan pulled up in front of Jessup's small, tidy wood-frame home at a few minutes after seven. It was pleasantly situated on a small pond, just a mile outside the lively, tourist-friendly town of Saranac Lake. The setting felt worlds away from Pike Hollow, with its sense of remote desolation amid an unending universe of dark malignant forest.

The house was decorated as Logan had expected: simple, Craftsman-style furniture; framed landscapes by local painters; a coffee table littered with the odd dichotomy of philosophical journals and magazines devoted to outdoor living. Over an excellent dinner of boeuf bourguignon and scalloped potatoes with raclette, he became acquainted with Jessup's pair of towheaded children and Suzanne, a lovely woman with an acerbic wit that

Logan hadn't expected. Before marrying Jessup, she had attended Radcliffe, then taught at the Friends Seminary, the old, prestigious private school in Manhattan. Academically, she was clearly a good match for his old friend the philosopher-cum-ranger, and though Logan privately wondered if she found enough to keep her intellectually stimulated in this sleepy backwoods community, she apparently had her hands full homeschooling their kids as well as doing volunteer tutoring of disadvantaged children around the area.

Dinner finished, Logan declined a slice of red velvet cake and, coffee cup in hand, followed Jessup out onto the front porch, where they sat in the inevitable Adirondack chairs and looked out over the pond. The windows threw cheerful yellow stripes of light out across the lawn, and the night was alive with the drone of insects. A waxing moon, almost full, shed a pale illumination over the surrounding forest.

Jessup took a sip of coffee, then set the cup down on the broad arm of his chair. "So," he said. "What did you think of Pike Hollow?"

"Wouldn't be my first choice to retire to."

Jessup smiled a little wryly. "Let me guess. The people you spoke with didn't agree with the official conclusion that we're dealing with a rogue bear."

"No. They had their own ideas about the responsible party."

"Let me guess once again—the Blakeney clan."

"That's right. I went to pay a visit on them before heading back. Got a twelve-gauge in the face for my trouble."

"I wish you hadn't gone there. You're lucky that's all you got." Jessup was silent for a moment. "It's my experience there's a short list of reasons why people live within the park. The first is that they were born here, it's all they know, and they have no desire or aspiration to move beyond it. The second is the tourist who comes here, falls in love, and either retires to the area or opens a shop or B and B or the like. Then there's the third reason. It's the person who doesn't feel he fits in today's society; that he is out of place, walking through life half asleep. People like that are drawn to the Adirondacks because, in Thoreau's words, they want to live *deliberately,* to 'front only the essential facts of life.' "

" 'The world is too much with us,' " Logan quoted. " 'Little we see in Nature that is ours.' "

"And Wordsworth had the right idea. But in any case, some people in this third group do tend to be a little crazy. Face it: one reason to live deep in the woods, away from other people, would be defective socialization. So, yes, as a ranger I've heard of many odd people living off by themselves in various degrees of rustication. Such people tend to attract speculation and rumor—it's only natural." He took a sip of his coffee. "But the Blakeneys are a special case."

Logan remained silent, letting his old friend talk.

"I've known about them for years, of course, but it wasn't until after the death of the second backpacker that I began actively looking into their history. People in Pike Hollow say they've always been there, and the official records show nothing to the contrary: their compound had already been in place for decades, at least, before the park's founding in 1885. All the park officials leave them alone, perhaps fearing that a confrontation would lead to some Waco-like tragedy. Their compound has never been officially surveyed, but that entire section of woods southwest of Pike Hollow has been grandfathered to the clan. No assessment has ever been made or taxes levied."

"I see."

"Of course, the Pike Hollow residents view the Blakeneys with the most suspicion, living as close to them as they do. There have been reports that others have had some limited success in getting acquainted. But there is no doubt they are an inbred, secretive, and most likely paranoid extended family, whose isolation over so many years has led to a warped view of the outside world." Jessup hesitated a moment before continuing. "Did any of the Pike Hollow people you spoke to talk of, ah, specifics?"

"Not really. The most they would do was lay the killings at the doorstep of the Blakeneys. The bar owner, Fred, said more than anybody." Logan pulled out his notebook, consulted it for a moment. "He said they had lived in the woods too long. He said doing that changes a person. He claimed they stole babies for unknown rituals. And he said they had unnatural dealings with the animals of the deep forest—that they had, in his words, tainted blood."

"Tainted blood," Jessup murmured. "Jeremy, let me explain something to you. That's about as far as you'd expect a citizen of Pike Hollow to open up to an outsider like yourself. But what they talk of among themselves is something else again. I know, because I've heard some of it."

"Such as?"

"Well, Fred Bridger was right. A few babies have gone missing over the last several decades. There have been several unexplained deaths in the park over the last forty years, and a disproportionate number of them happened in the Five Ponds vicinity. For a long time now—even though they wouldn't say it to your face—the inhabitants around those parts think they know *exactly* what the Blakeneys are . . . and what kind of changes they've experienced."

Jessup took another sip of coffee. The droning of insects increased.

"Well?" Logan spoke into the silence. "What do the inhabitants think the Blakeneys are?"

"Lycanthropes." Jessup spoke the word carefully, as if tasting it.

"Lycanthropes?" Logan repeated. "People believe the Blakeney clan to be *werewolves*? That's—"

"What? Ridiculous? Coming from an enigmalogist like you?"

"But there's no clinical evidence to support such a phenomenon. A human being, transforming into a wolf?"

"From what I've read, you've investigated stranger things than that. And don't forget, these are people who know the Blakeneys best—who have lived, practically on their doorstep, for generations. They've seen things that you and I haven't."

Logan glanced at the ranger with fresh surprise. Was it possible Jessup might actually lend credence to such a story?

Jessup, looking over, guessed what Logan was thinking. He smiled again the thoughtful, wistful smile Logan remembered so well.

"Now you know why I asked you to go out to Pike Hollow today—and why you were the only person I *could* ask. I mean, let's face it—it's your job."

This was true, Logan admitted to himself; as an enigmalogist, he couldn't discount any possibility. And Jessup knew these woods and these people much better than he did.

"I'm not saying I believe it," Jessup went on. "I'm not saying that at all. But as a ranger, I can't just ignore it, either. Rumors don't just start themselves. And a lot of strange things are hidden away in these six million acres of forest."

Logan didn't reply.

"Just give it some thought," Jessup said after a long silence. "And read those case files." And with that he drained his coffee cup, set it down again, and gazed out over the moonlit pond.

9

For the next two days, Logan remained cloistered in his cabin at Cloudwater. The days were Indian-summer warm and the nights brisk and clear. He found himself quickly slipping into a routine. He skipped breakfast, instead making himself a pot of coffee that he nursed over the course of the day. Lunch, always excellent, was brought to his cabin around one p.m. He left the cabin only to have dinner in the main lodge, where he became acquainted with the people staying in the cabins closest to his—a conceptual artist and a pianist-composer—and where talk lingered on the subjects of the weather and their individual projects.

Logan had feared it would take him some time to get reimmersed in his monograph, but Cloudwater seemed to exert an almost magical influence: the enforced isolation, and the faintly competitive awareness of all the work being done by others in the cabins around him, sharpened his concentration. By the end of the first day, he had acquainted himself once again with the source material and reread what he'd accomplished so far; by the end of the second, he was actively writing. It was this sense of real progress that, after dinner that second night, allowed him to relax his guard and finally take a look at Jessup's case files.

The clinical details in the files did not add much to what he already knew about the murders—except for their sheer ferocity, which was obvious from the evidence photos even given the advanced states of decomposition. While the bodies had not been eaten, they had been torn apart with remarkable fury. The corpses were too far gone for the wounds themselves to be analyzed with any accuracy, and it was primarily the brute strength necessary to rend a human body in such a way that caused the ME to presume bear attacks.

The other commonalities he already knew: both victims were backpackers, both had been killed in the vicinity of Desolation Mountain, and both had been killed during full moons.

Pushing the case files away, Logan accessed the Internet and spent ninety minutes researching werewolves. The situation he found himself in was, he realized, a little unusual. While over the course of his career he had looked into all sorts of so-called monsters—mummies, revenants, and the rest of the Hollywood horror-movie parade—he had never dealt with werewolves. Zombies could be explained away by the absorption of tetrodotoxin-laced *coupe poudre* into the bloodstream; belief in vampirism was said by some to be based on victims of porphyria, or mass hysteria of the sort found following the death of the so-called Serbian vampire Petar Blagojevich. And yet werewolves had always seemed—from a scientific aspect—the least explainable to him. And he found nothing on the web to change his mind. He was aware, of course, of clinical lycanthropy—the delusional, even schizophrenic, belief that a person could transform himself into an animal. He also knew something of hypertrichosis, or "werewolf syndrome," in which victims are afflicted with excessive and abnormal hair growth, sometimes covering the entire body. Yet neither of these fit the true definition of a werewolf: a human with the ability to shape-shift into a vicious, wolflike creature.

Still, there was no denying that the werewolf legend was both remarkably old and remarkably tenacious, having its roots in ancient Greece and coming to full flower in Central Europe during the Middle Ages. And there it continued to persist in the years that followed: in such books as Claude Prieur's 1596 *Dialogue de la lycanthropie,* or 1621's *Anatomy of Melancholy,* in which Robert Burton devoted an entire subchapter to lycanthropia, or "wolf-madness"—supposedly caused by an excess of melancholic humor—in which the sufferer believed himself to be a wolf. Even John Webster allowed Duke Ferdinand, a villain in his infamously blood-drenched play *The Duchess of Malfi,* to succumb to the malady:

> They imagine
> Themselves to be transformèd into wolves;
> Steal forth to church-yards in the dead of night,
> And dig dead bodies up: as two nights since
> One met the Duke 'bout midnight in a lane
> Behind Saint Mark's Church, with the leg of a man
> Upon his shoulder, and he howl'd fearfully;
> Said he was a wolf—only the difference

Was, a wolf's skin was hairy on the outside,
His on the inside.

In the Elizabethan-era firsthand accounts Logan managed to
unearth, werewolves or wolf-men were usually the result of dab-
blings in witchcraft, or at times the direct intervention of Satan
himself. One such tract, "A true Discourse. Declaring the dam-
nable life and death of one Stubbe Peeter, a most wicked Sor-
cerer, who in the likenes of a woolfe, committed many murders,"
described an evil man who—thanks to the practice of sorcery—
could turn into a wolf almost at will, and whose favorite practice
included accosting pregnant women, "tearing the Children out of
their wombes, in most bloody and savedge sorte, and after eate
their hartes panting hotte and rawe."

Indeed, the accounts and descriptions he examined differed
in precisely how, when, and why lycanthropes turned from men
to wolves, as well as how much control they had over the process.
One thing, however, most sources agreed on: werewolves were at
their most powerful, most bestial, and least able to govern their
savage impulses on the nights of a full moon.

Logan closed his laptop with a sigh. By definition, his job as
an enigmalogist meant he needed to keep an open mind about
anything, no matter how strange; his resistance, even skepticism,
about the possibility of a phenomenon like lycanthropy was something he couldn't explain.

Feeling the need for a breath of air, he left his cabin, then
wandered down the pathways in the direction of the main lodge.
Almost all its hundred-odd windows gleamed with warm yellow
light, and voices could be heard faintly on the autumn breeze: no
doubt the question-and-answer session following that evening's

colloquium. Logan couldn't help contrasting the inviting cheer of this vast building to the ancient, haunted, and forbidding structure he had seen rising up beyond the barricade surrounding the Blakeney compound.

Emerging onto the broad lawn, he made his way down to the lake. Here, the voices were out of earshot, and the only sounds he heard were the lapping of water by his feet and the restless night noises of the forest insects. The moon, just grown full, hung low over the water, so large it seemed almost within his grasp.

The sounds of quiet footsteps approached through the grass behind him, and then came a voice: "Good evening to you, Dr. Logan."

Logan turned. It was Hartshorn, the resident director.

"To you as well. And it is a beautiful evening."

"This is my favorite time of year. Warm days, cool nights. Great sleeping weather. The summer tourists have left, and the skiers haven't yet arrived." The moon lit up the director's mane of white hair with an almost ghostly glow. "How is your work going?"

"Remarkably well. With the progress I'm making, I might cut short my stay."

"We can't have that." And Hartshorn smiled. He seemed more at ease than he had during their first meeting. Clearly, the low profile Logan had been keeping was putting the director at ease.

"I understand that ranger visited you the night you arrived," Hartshorn said, with deliberate casualness.

This fellow doesn't miss much. "Like I told you, he and I go way back."

"You went to Yale together, you said." Hartshorn shook his head. "A Yale-educated ranger. Interesting."

"Well, let's call him a born philosopher who happens to spend his days as a ranger."

Hartshorn chuckled. "So he just stopped by to catch up."

Logan understood the inference immediately: Hartshorn knew about the murders of the backpackers, of course, and he was wondering if—for whatever reason—the ranger who had seemed so eager to see him was enlisting his help. "I haven't seen him for many years," he said. "A lot of water under the bridge."

Hartshorn merely nodded.

It might, Logan realized, be a good idea to throw the director a bone. After all, if he displayed no interest in local folklore at all, it would seem so out of character as to raise Hartshorn's suspicions—and the last thing he wanted was to have his comings and goings monitored. "Randall has seen a lot during his years as a ranger," he said. "It seems the residents of these woods have more than their share of tall tales."

"Which would naturally be of interest to you—given your avocation, I mean. Well, I've never had much to do with the locals, but I do know enough to take their tall tales with a huge grain of salt. No objectivity, you know. Except for Albright, I suppose."

"I'm sorry?"

"Harrison Albright. Well-respected poet. Grew up in the park, then moved away as a teenager. Came back here in the late nineties and has made the Adirondacks his home ever since. You won't find him passing on rumors or giving credence to legends. He's giving a lecture here next week, in fact. You might enjoy hearing him talk."

"I'll be sure to do that. Thanks."

"Well, enjoy the rest of your evening. And good luck with the monograph." Hartshorn smiled once again, then turned and made his way back in the direction of the lodge.

10

After lunch the following day, Logan did not return to his monograph. Instead, he called a cab, walked down Cloudwater's private drive to the main road, and had himself driven into Saranac Lake, where he rented a Jeep Wrangler. His own car was scratched and muddy from the trip to the Blakeney compound, and he wasn't about to risk more serious damage on future outings. Besides, the Wrangler would be less conspicuous.

While completing the rental paperwork, Logan asked the clerk offhandedly about Harrison Albright. Not only did the man know of the poet, but he knew precisely where he lived. It was as Hartshorn had told him: for all its size, the Adirondacks sometimes felt like a small community. And so, on the drive back from Saranac Lake, Logan passed right by the entrance to Cloudwater and instead continued on down 3, then off onto 3A once again, looking for a particular A-frame with a red Ford F1 in the driveway, a mile or two short of the Pike Hollow turnoff. It was ironic, Logan thought: in the very act of trying to keep him at Cloudwater, busily working on his monograph, Hartshorn had instead—by mentioning Albright—unwittingly helped him decide on the next move in his investigation.

Late that morning, Logan had walked over to the lodge and availed himself of Cloudwater's generous and wide-ranging library. Among the many titles he found several volumes of Albright's poetry: *From the Deep Woods; Algonquin Peak; The Mossy Col.* Leafing through them, he found verses of an accessible, rough-hewn character that nevertheless showed considerable craftsmanship and native skill. Some of the poems were musings on Adirondack life; others were rustic ballad tales of the Robert W. Service and John Masefield school. The brief bio on the back cover of one of the books burbled that Albright was "a modern-day Davy Crockett" who had been born "with maple syrup in his veins."

Making this particular drive for the second time, Logan was again conscious of leaving what passed for civilization and heading into the dark heart of an immense, untamed, uncaring wilderness. It was odd: his job as an enigmalogist had taken him to far more remote places in the past—Alaska's Federal Wildlife Zone, hundreds of miles north of the Arctic Circle; the vast swampy wasteland south of Egypt known as the Sudd—and yet none of these had filled him with the kind of vague anxiety that he felt now, driving once more toward the hamlet of Pike Hollow and, beyond it, the strange wall of twigs that hid the Blakeney compound from the outside world.

He rounded a bend and the A-frame, with its red pickup, came into view on the right. Logan slowed, then turned into the short driveway. The house was set back about a hundred feet from the road and—while not as trim and shiny as the Jessup residence—was in relatively good repair. A large woodpile was set beneath a shelter beside the pickup, and gray smoke was curling up from the redbrick chimney. There was no backyard to speak of; the woods crowded in on three sides.

Getting out of the Jeep, Logan walked down a rough path half covered in pine needles, mounted the steps, and—seeing there was no doorbell—rapped on the front door. A moment of silence, and then he heard a stirring within and the door opened. A man of about sixty stared out at him from the darkness of the house: tall and muscular, with penetrating blue eyes, close-cropped white hair, and an equally white beard that spread out to cover his entire jawline. He wore a plaid work shirt and faded denims, and a long knife sheath of scuffed leather hung from his belt. He said nothing, but merely raised his bushy eyebrows questioningly.

Only now did Logan realize that—most uncharacteristically—he had not prepared for this visit. He'd surmised, from Hartshorn's comments, that Albright's opinion on the recent killings might be worth hearing—but he had not given thought as to how he should present himself to the man or approach the subject. He'd simply been too preoccupied, feeling the forest close in around him as he drove west from Saranac Lake, to do this most basic bit of social engineering. He'd have to wing it.

"Mr. Albright?" he asked.

The man nodded.

"I wonder if I might come in for a minute."

Still the man looked at him impassively.

"I'm not selling anything. The name's Logan."

"I know who you are," the man said at last in a gravelly baritone. "I saw that special on the Discovery Channel—the one where you disproved the existence of the Loch Ness Monster. I'm just not sure I want to let you in."

Now it was Logan's turn to look quizzical.

"I can guess why you're here. I love these woods—and I don't want to have them tainted by a lot of bad publicity."

I see, Logan thought. "Would it help if I told you I'm staying at Cloudwater, putting the finishing touches on a historical essay? I'm not here to generate PR, good or bad. In fact, I'm doing my best to stay below the radar. Fact is, the Cloudwater director would be very upset if he knew I was even here."

The man considered. Then his creased face broke into a smile. "Okay," he said. "I'm speaking there next week, and if this conversation ends up with me not liking you, I'll rat you out."

"Fair enough," Logan said, unable to suppress a faint sense of misgiving.

The man stood back and let Logan into a small living room, furnished in a simple, almost spartan style. Much of the furniture seemed handmade. There was a makeshift bookcase, full of all manner of titles; a writing desk; some wooden chairs; and a standing lamp with the usual birch-bark lampshade.

Albright motioned Logan to a chair, straight-backed and uncomfortable. "Beer?"

"No thanks."

"Good, 'cause there are only two left in the fridge and I don't feel like driving into town for more." The man eased himself down into another chair with a sigh. "Now, why don't you tell me just what I can do for you?"

"Before we get into that, I have a question. It seems you already know who I am. Can you tell me a bit about yourself?"

Albright shrugged. "Not that much to tell. I was born just ten miles from here. My old man was in the logging business. Taught me all he knew about woodcraft. Died in an accident when I was fourteen. My mother couldn't wait to get me and my brother out of the backwoods. We moved to Albany so I could get what she called a 'real education.' Went to University of Albany, SUNY. While there, I got interested in literature, especially poetry. Worked a bunch of different jobs downstate and wrote poetry in the evenings. Finally got my first book, *Trailhead,* published. Made just enough money so I could move back here—like I'd always wanted to do." He got up, walked out of the room, came back a minute later with a bottle of beer in his hand. "Good enough?"

"Thank you."

Albright sat down again and took a pull from the bottle. "Now, maybe you can tell me just how you became a . . . what was that term they used in the documentary?"

"Enigmalogist. Well, in my case you start by reading every ghost story you can get your hands on when you're very young and warp your mind in the process. Then you supplement that with *Stranger Than Science.* And then you start actively searching out real-life enigmas. It wasn't anything I planned, really—I just fell into it." Logan shrugged. "A hundred years ago, there were lots of sensational mysteries written about ghost-breakers and occult detectives and the like. Today, it's kind of a specialized field."

Albright nodded, took another sip of beer.

Logan had made up his mind to be a little coy with the poet, but realized he was dealing with a shrewd, intelligent man and that the best course would probably be to level with him. "I'll tell you exactly why I'm here. A friend of mine—a forest ranger—

heard that I was staying at Cloudwater. He asked me to look into the recent deaths of the two backpackers over by Desolation Mountain. He doesn't seem convinced by the official account that the two men were killed by bears."

Albright nodded again. He didn't look surprised.

"I've talked to the residents of the nearby town, Pike Hollow. They don't believe bears were at fault, either. They seem to blame the Blakeney clan. And—I've been told—they believe the Blakeneys are . . . well . . . werewolves."

Albright's expression didn't change. He merely studied the label on his beer bottle.

"And then I heard about you. You were somebody who had grown up here, an Adirondacks native, knew the backwoods like the palm of your hand. But you'd also lived away long enough to gain some objectivity." Logan hesitated. "In my field, I'm supposed to keep an open mind about everything. But to be honest, I'm having a difficult time wrapping my head around this. Werewolves . . . Anyway, I just wanted to know what your opinion was."

"My opinion." Albright put the bottle of beer on the floor beside his chair. "I guess I can sum that up easily enough, too. Logan, I can understand your skepticism. I've heard some pretty outrageous tales myself in the twenty years since I've moved back. But I'll tell you something—something you may already know, given your particular line of work. Many times, legends—no matter how outlandish they sound—have a grounding in reality. And in a place as remote and old as the Adirondacks, it may well be that there are phenomena that cold, twenty-first-century rationality can't fully explain—or even comprehend."

"In other words, just because I think the opinion of the locals is outlandish, that doesn't mean I should ignore it."

Albright nodded.

"What about you? Do *you* believe the Blakeneys are responsible? Do you believe they could possibly be werewolves?"

Albright chuckled. Then he shook his head, spread his hands. "In the backwoods of the Adirondacks, Dr. Logan, there's history—and then there's mystery. I think I'll get you that beer, after all."

Two hours later, just as the sun was setting and darkness crept over the woods, Logan said good-bye to Albright and got into his rented Jeep. Unable to get any further answers out of the man, Logan had continued chatting with him anyway, and soon found that—beneath the gruff, even coarse exterior—lay an intellect both keen and highly observant. It was interesting, he thought as he started the engine and pulled back onto Route 3A, how different the fellow was from Jessup. A lot of this, he supposed, could be traced to the fact that Albright was a true mountain man, who had grown up deep in the Adirondacks and who, despite his mother's attempt to get him a "real education," had clearly never lost the backwoods skills—or, in some ways, the outlook—ingrained in him by his father. Jessup, on the other hand, had spent his childhood in outlying Plattsburgh. The difference could be summed up in the ways the two men viewed nature. Jessup, the Ivy League philosopher, looked at it through Thoreauvian eyes: a cosmic leveler of humanity, something one could hold up as a mirror to the way we should live and view our fellow man. Albright, on the other hand, seemed to look at it in much the way his father must have: something to be experienced and enjoyed, but also an elemental force to be respected . . . and, when necessary, feared.

Just at that moment, his cell phone rang. Logan plucked it from his pocket. "Yes?"

"Jeremy?" came the faint, crackly voice. "It's Randall. Where are you?"

"I'm driving back to Cloudwater."

"I've been trying to get ahold of you for the last fifteen minutes. How soon will you be there?"

"I guess I was out of cell reception. Less than half an hour. Why?"

"There's been another killing."

Logan felt himself grip the phone tighter. "Like the others?"

"Apparently so. I'm heading there now. Step on it—I'll pick you up on my way past." The connection went dead.

Logan slipped the phone thoughtfully back into his pocket. Then he glanced out the window, looking skyward through the thick tangle of tree branches. A full moon, bloated and pale yellow, stared back at him, unblinking.

11

Logan had grabbed a duffel bag from his cabin and met Jessup out at the entrance to Cloudwater, eager to avoid offering its residents the spectacle of an official vehicle with a flashing lightbar. Jessup drove fast down the twisting highway, headlights stabbing into the unrelieved darkness. Infrequently, a small blur of habitation would shoot past the windows. In the indirect dashboard illumination, the ranger's face was set in a grim mask. He turned down one dirt road, and then another, and Logan quickly grew disoriented by the walls of dark trunks flashing past, the canopy of branches overhead. The cabin of the vehicle was silent save for the occasional squawk of the police radio.

"Where was the body found?" Logan asked at last.

"Near Sand Creek. A hunter found it, traveling along a private inholding on an ATV."

"Backpacker?"

"I don't know."

"Near Desolation Mountain?"

"Closer. Five Ponds Wilderness, maybe four miles from Pike Hollow."

Now Jessup turned off the road onto something that could barely be called a trail, the heavy truck bouncing and floundering wildly over exposed roots and deep ruts, pushing tall grass and saplings out of the way. Ahead, Logan could make out a faint, flickering glow.

And then, quite suddenly, the forest gave way to a clearing. Just before them was a cluster of vehicles—state police cars, Forest Preserve trucks, an ambulance—parked in a rough semicircle, engines running, headlights converging on a single spot. Jessup slowed, then pulled in beside the closest vehicle.

"Stay in the background," he told Logan. "But keep your eyes and ears open."

Jessup got out, and Logan followed him as he walked behind the parked vehicles to a spot where about a dozen men were clustered, speaking together in low tones. Another man, apparently a scene-of-crime officer, was unspooling yellow tape around the large perimeter on which the headlights had converged. The full, bloated moon hung over all.

"CSI?" Jessup asked a fellow ranger.

"Inbound from Plattsburgh. Expected at any moment."

"Any idea how long the body's been dead?"

"The ME will give us specifics, but I'd guess twenty-four hours, max."

"Identification?" Jessup asked.

"Nobody's touching that body until CSI gets here." This was spoken by a state trooper with two silver bars on his uniform: a large, burly, no-nonsense man who appeared to be in charge. The trooper looked at Jessup's fellow ranger, then at Jessup, and then at Logan, who was hanging back in Jessup's shadow. He glared for a minute, then turned back to the man he'd been talking to: a pudgy, white-faced man in a faded army jacket that, Logan assumed, was the person who had found the victim.

Logan looked over at the body, illuminated in the pitiless beams of the headlights, then after a few brief seconds quickly looked away again. He had seen death before, of course, on numerous occasions, but he had never seen a corpse so violently torn and lacerated. What had once been clothes were now mere strips of blood-soaked ribbons, decorating the surrounding plants like so much crimson confetti. The limbs were broken and cocked at strange angles. Viscera had been pulled from the body cavity and strewn about seemingly at random, soaking the ground in black blood and leaving the chest and peritoneum an empty shell. The face was so shredded as to be unrecognizable.

Sickened, he fell back farther, returned to Jessup's truck, and stared out at the surrounding landscape. After the bright beams of the headlights, the night forest seemed blacker than ever. He wasn't sure, but it appeared that the woods beyond the clearing were thinner here. *The Five Ponds Wilderness* . . . Logan wondered just how far they were from the Blakeney compound.

Circling around Jessup's truck, he made his way over the dark and treacherous ground until he came to the edge of the crime scene tape, on the far side from where the others stood, talking quietly. When he was sure the group was ignoring him, he let his duffel slip to the ground and unzipped it. Then he reached in and removed a small device with a digital readout, toggle switches, and a fat adjustable knob: an air ion counter. He held the device out at arm's length, then swept it in an arc around him, adjusting the knob as he did so. The reading here was barely different from the basal reading he'd taken upon first arriving at Cloudwater: the air ionization was greater by less than 250 ions per cm^3. He would also take readings at Pike Hollow and the entrance to the Blakeney compound when he had the chance, but he doubted they would be any more conclusive.

Returning the device to his duffel, he took out another: a tri-field EM detector. Once again, he swung the detector in an arc, at last pointing it in the direction of the body and holding it there, carefully observing the analog needle on its VU gauge as he did so. Once again, the readings were inconclusive.

The equipment told him what he had already anticipated. This was not the site of spectral or paranormal activity: what had happened here was all too physical; all too corporeal—the body on the ground before him was bloody, violent proof of that.

Putting the EM detector back into the duffel and zipping it closed, he remained at the periphery of the crime scene tape, still facing the body. As a "sensitive," a natural empath, he not only had a heightened ability to sense the emotions and feelings of other people, but he could, sometimes, gather a feeling of a *place,* as well. Normally, this happened when a presence, usually evil, had dwelt in one spot for a long time. However, it was occasionally possible that, when great evil or violence had visited a location even briefly, a vestigial sense of that evil remained—temporarily. Now he closed his eyes, emptying himself of thought and emotion, shutting out the murmur of voices, letting the darkness that surrounded him creep into his mind, waiting for the surroundings, for the dead body splayed before him, to speak; to render up their secrets; to let him know something of what had transpired here.

For several moments he simply stood, mind empty, waiting. And then—abruptly—he went rigid. And he remained so for over a minute until, with a wail of sirens, a paramedic van and two red-painted SUVs—no doubt the CSI team—arrived on scene.

Logan barely noticed. He opened his eyes, and his shoulders slumped wearily. Picking up the duffel, he made his way back to Jessup's truck, where he got in to await the ranger's return. He had seen—and sensed—enough for one night.

Because, standing there before the scene of almost unimaginable violence, he had gathered one sensation—and one only. There was a wrongness to this place: something that he could not understand or even begin to fully apprehend. The killer, he sensed, was human—and yet, at the same time, *not human*.

12

The New York State Forest Rangers Headquarters, Region 5, was an unprepossessing, cinder-block, two-story affair on the outskirts of Ray Brook. It was a few minutes before eleven the following morning when Jessup met Logan at the entrance to the HQ, brought him inside, and took him upstairs to a conference room. It was full of rangers all wearing their distinctive hats, rubbing shoulders with uniformed state police along with a few people in mufti. Jessup introduced him to a tall, muscularly built man whom he identified as Jack Cornhill, supervisor, Zone C, then steered him to a seat in the back of the room.

"I thought I was supposed to keep a low profile," Logan said. "Here you're ushering me into the lion's den."

"Chance I had to take," Jessup replied, taking the seat beside him. "The ME's about to give his report. If anybody asks, just offer up some vague double-talk about research you're doing for Yale. And do your best to keep away from Krenshaw."

"Krenshaw?"

Jessup nodded toward the podium, beside which stood the burly state policeman Logan had seen at the crime scene the night before.

"Captain Krenshaw," Jessup said. "Zone commander, Troop B. His troop covers most of the Adirondacks. As I told you, the whole region is awash in overlapping jurisdictions. But with three unsolved killings now, Krenshaw is sure to take command. He's a downstater, born and raised on Long Island."

"How'd he end up here?"

"You'd have to ask the troop commander that. Anyway, Krenshaw is a typical state policeman. He came up through the ranks. Has the imaginative capacity of a snapping turtle. You can guess the dim view he'd take of the rumors you've been looking into."

There was a sudden flurry of activity at the front of the room and a short woman in slacks and a white blouse walked up to the podium, then tapped on the microphone.

"Alice Hannigan," Jessup whispered to Logan as he pulled out his journal in preparation for taking notes. "Captain of Region Five. She's the ranger in charge of all eight northern counties."

"May I have your attention," Hannigan said briskly. "We'll do our best to keep this short. I'll give you a few preliminary facts. Then we will hear a brief overview from Dr. Bryce Plowson, the Plattsburgh ME, regarding the autopsy of the latest victim. Finally, Captain Krenshaw of the New York state police will discuss the investigative procedures to be followed, going forward."

She cleared her throat, glanced over a few index cards. "The victim has been identified as one Mark Artowsky, twenty-two years of age. When discovered, he had been dead approximately eighteen hours. He was a graduate student, working with a small research team operating out of a disused fire station at the southern edge of the Five Ponds Wilderness. As you know, unlike the two backpackers whose remains were discovered previously, Artowsky was found along the eastern fringe of the Wilderness, about six miles north of the weather station and not quite four miles southwest of Pike Hollow. Any questions?"

When there were none, she yielded the podium to a bald elderly man with heavy spectacles, wearing a white coat over a dark suit. He adjusted the microphone, looked around. "I'll spare you as much of the medical technicalities as I can," he said in a high, reedy voice. "First, the good news. As Captain Hannigan has just told you, the body was found relatively soon after death. This meant that a much more accurate autopsy could be performed than on the two men found earlier. Unfortunately, despite that fact, much about this death remains inconclusive."

Dr. Plowson took a sip of water from a glass at one side of the podium. "Put quite simply, although the attack was just as ferocious and violent as the first two corpses indicated, the size of the puncture marks, and the depth of the wounds, are not sufficiently large as to indicate a bear. A more likely animal would be a gray wolf."

A wolf. Beside him, Logan felt Jessup stiffen.

"The size and distribution of the puncture marks, along with the uninhibited bite pattern around the neck, are consistent with that of a wolf. The puncture wounds were created no doubt by the maxillae, which then—as is common in dog or wolf attacks—served as anchor points for the tearing that follows when the attacking animal shakes its victim. Unfortunately, there is a shortage of literature regarding specific analyses and comparison of lupine dentition and claw marks, so the assessment that a wolf made these bites cannot be one hundred percent conclusive. Besides which, the body is simply in too great a state of dismemberment for the recovery of any paw marks. And it is precisely that dismemberment which adds a further complication to forensic analysis. Normally, a wolf attack—in cases, at least, where extreme aggravation or the protection of cubs was not an underlying cause—would be followed by postmortem feeding. That was not the case here. Instead, the victim's limbs were severed from the torso with great violence—and in a way inconsistent with the kind of biting, rending behavior we would normally expect from a wolf attack. In addition, the evisceration of the body cavity is extremely unusual. Odontological analysis of the wounds to the limbs and viscera would be helpful, of course, but given the victim's condition it is almost impossible to establish a useful bite mark protocol."

Standing beside the medical examiner, Captain Krenshaw stirred. "Excuse me, Doctor," he said. "Am I to understand, then, that certain aspects of this attack are consistent with that of a wolf, while others are completely inconsistent?"

"That is correct," Dr. Plowson said. "As I mentioned, the concentrated bite pattern around the neck, and the nature of the puncture wounds, are typical. And yet many things—the mauling of the body, the blunt trauma inflicted upon it, the evisceration, and the lack of postmortem feeding—are not typical of a wolf at all and, in fact, are difficult if not impossible to explain."

"Could not these wounds have been inflicted by a man, using a weapon such as a butcher's cleaver, or maybe a winnowing fork?"

The ME pushed his glasses up his nose. "That might account

for the lacerations, the way the body was for all purposes torn apart, but of course it would not explain the bite patterns."

"Unless the man in question made the bite marks himself," Krenshaw said. "Thank you, Doctor. Was there anything else?"

"Not at this time. If anything further comes to light, I'll be sure to let you know."

Krenshaw nodded, then let the doctor step aside and assumed the podium himself. "All right. From what Dr. Plowson has told us, we can't rule anything out—animal or human. With this third murder, we now have no choice but to search these woods with a fine-tooth comb. Captain Hannigan of the rangers will coordinate that search. You'll need to concentrate on the Five Ponds Wilderness and the area around Desolation Mountain. Given the lengthy periods between the killings and the discoveries of the first two bodies, not to mention the conditions of the terrain, previous searches were minimal. That won't be the case this time. I'll call in helicopter support to assist. Despite what we've heard, be prepared for anything—bear *or* wolf. Meanwhile, the troopers under my command will investigate the possibility that a human perpetrator is involved. We will interview the local residents, look for criminal histories, interface with Dannemorra prison regarding any recent parolees, and search for any commonalities. Troopers, you'll be taking your specific instructions from your station commanders and zone sergeants. Any questions? No? Very good. This meeting is adjourned."

As the rangers and state police began rising and murmuring among themselves, Logan watched Krenshaw leave the podium and—looking straight at him—make his way through the rows of chairs.

"Uh-oh," he murmured to Jessup. "Care to do the talking?"

Captain Krenshaw stopped directly before Logan, meaty arms crossed over his chest. "What are you doing here, exactly?"

Logan took a breath. "I'm a historical researcher from Yale, investigating—"

"Academics aren't invited to official briefings such as this." Krenshaw smiled mirthlessly. Despite his girth, he had remarkably tiny, deep-set eyes that had the uncomfortable ability to bore into a person. "Besides, I know all about your researches, *Doctor* Logan. I've seen your face on TV more than once. And I can guess why you're here—I've heard some of the talk coming out of Pike Hollow, too. If you want my own opinion, you're wasting your time. This wasn't the work of an animal, and it sure as hell wasn't the work of a monster. In fact, I've got a pretty good idea who's responsible."

"And who would that be?" Jessup asked.

"Saul Woden." Now Krenshaw turned to the ranger. "As for you, Lieutenant Jessup, I'm making it your responsibility to see to it that Logan here doesn't interfere—*and* doesn't attract unwanted publicity. He is not to involve himself with the official investigation in any way. Is that clear?"

"Quite," said Jessup.

Krenshaw looked from Jessup to Logan, then back again. And then, without another word, he turned away and moved toward a cluster of state police near the front of the room.

Jessup sighed, stood up. Logan did the same.

"Who's Saul Woden?" Logan asked.

"No idea. But I think we'd better get you out of the building before Krenshaw has you bodily ejected." Jessup shook his head. "Sorry about that."

"Don't be. I've got a paper waiting for me back at Cloudwater . . . and some catching up to do."

He let Jessup show him out, then walked to his rented Jeep, started the engine, and began heading back toward Cloudwater. But even as he did so—even as he began trying to compose his thoughts for work on his monograph—he could not get the words of the medical examiner out of his head:

Much about this death remains inconclusive . . . A likely animal would be a gray wolf . . . And yet many things are not typical of a wolf at all and, in fact, are difficult if not impossible to explain.

13

It was three days before Logan next called Jessup.

"Jeremy. Hey. I thought maybe Krenshaw had scared you off."

"I just wanted to lie low until things calmed down a little. Have they?"

"Calmed down? No. But they've grown a little more organized. Krenshaw and his boys have begun interviewing all the local populace. It hasn't gone down very well, I can tell you that much."

"Has he tried to interview the Blakeneys?"

"He tried, yes. Apparently he didn't get any farther than you did. I don't know how the exchange went, exactly, but he seems to have backed off for the time being. Posted a trooper at the entrance to their compound. Talked about sending in a surveillance drone." Jessup chuckled his mirthless laugh.

"What about the search teams?"

"They've been mustered. Helicopter-assisted searches of Five Ponds and the Desolation Lake region are under way now."

"Any luck?"

"Nothing yet except a lot of blistered feet, two sprained ankles, and a vicious case of poison ivy."

"Why aren't you using dogs?"

Another mirthless laugh. "They're useless on this search. They just clamp their tails between their legs and whine. Refuse to track."

Logan thought a moment. "What about the research team this dead graduate student worked with? Are they still part of the active investigation?"

"No. Krenshaw was in and out of their camp on the day of the briefing. Spent a couple of hours questioning them. With Artowsky's death, there are only two people left there now. Frankly, I'm surprised they didn't pack up and leave months ago, under the circumstances."

"So I could pay a visit without attracting official attention?" Logan thought he would try to determine the "circumstances" for himself.

"I think so. Not sure how much you'll learn, if anything, but I'm glad you're still interested in looking into it."

As it happened, Logan wasn't particularly interested in looking into it. Ironically, it was his own skepticism about the local belief in lycanthropy that was pushing him to follow up every avenue; if he didn't, he knew he'd be doing himself, and his unusual profession, a disservice. So he got careful directions to the research outpost from Jessup and took off in his Jeep around ten in the morning.

He knew the first part of the route well enough now—Route

3 to Route 3A—and the long journey into the heart of the wild did not feel quite as disquieting as it had on previous occasions. He passed Pike Hollow; passed the turnoff to the Blakeney compound—with a state police vehicle parked on the shoulder beside it—and then left the seamed blacktop of 3A himself a mile farther on for one of the rutted, muddy, narrow dirt lanes that seemed to crisscross this region of the park. The road forked, then forked again, and despite Jessup's directions Logan got lost twice. Once, the dirt lane ended in a tangle of blowdowns and wild underbrush; another time, he realized that the road led back on itself and he'd gone in a circle. But at last he pulled the Jeep up to the one-acre clearing in the woods that housed the fire station. The station itself consisted of a ruined fire tower, once quite tall but now fallen in upon itself; a long, low fire command station at its base that resembled an oversized Quonset hut; a scattering of outbuildings; and a parking area housing two vehicles. A large commercial generator, fueled by a nearby five-thousand-gallon propane tank, grumbled away beside the Quonset hut. Off in the distance, a dog barked once.

Logan had done a little research into the history of Adirondack fire lookout towers. The first was built in 1909, after almost a million acres of forest had been ravaged by fire over the previous decade. In the years to come, almost sixty towers and, in many cases, attendant stations were erected. They remained in place for more than half a century before being replaced by newer technologies. A few dozen still remained in the region, some of them tourist attractions, some listed on the National Register of Historic Places, and others—such as this one—repurposed and given new life.

Getting out of his vehicle, he walked down the pebbled path to the old fire command station, apparently—judging by its relative state of repair and the satellite dish on its roof—the center of the scientific operation. He stepped up to the door, knocked.

A minute later, a young, slightly overweight man in a lab coat opened it. He had unkempt brown hair and brown, calflike eyes.

"Yes?" the man said, blinking at Logan.

"The name's Logan. Do you mind if I come in a minute?"

"Are you another policeman?" the man asked.

"No." Logan took the opportunity to slip past the man into the building. "What's your name?"

The man in the lab coat looked around the laboratory for a moment before replying. "Kevin Pace."

"Quite a place you have here," Logan said. And it was. The exterior's rustic, rather shabby appearance was a far cry from the inside, which appeared to be a cutting-edge laboratory. It sported three worktables covered with apparatus; several light boxes and a variety of optical equipment; a rack of computer servers and various scientific analyzers; rows of plastic cages for housing small animals; numerous tall storage shelves of gray metal, carefully labeled; a small dissection table; and what appeared to be a "clean room" set into one corner. There was a framed picture on the closest lab table: a young woman hugging an elderly, tall, white-haired man with a salt-and-pepper beard, standing in a brick quadrangle that reminded Logan of Oxford. On one wall was a bulletin board, numerous moths and butterflies pinned to it, along with notes covered in scrawled handwriting. There was a faint smell of formaldehyde in the air.

"How can I help you, exactly?" Pace asked.

"I'm a fellow scientist," Logan said. "Staying at Cloudwater—in the Thomas Cole cabin, as it happens—putting the finishing touches on a paper. I heard about your outpost, here in the middle of nowhere, and curiosity got the better of me."

"Okay," the young man said. Logan had already sensed he was withdrawn, timid, not one to readily volunteer information.

"I also wanted to express my condolences about the death of your coworker. How terrible."

Pace nodded.

"He was a fellow researcher, I understand?"

"Yes."

"And have you been here long?"

"About eight months. We were hired to work for Dr. Feverbridge."

"Feverbridge?" Logan asked. "Chase Feverbridge?"

Pace nodded again. He was looking more closely—and curiously—at Logan.

Logan had heard a little about Feverbridge. He was a brilliant, if highly iconoclastic, naturalist, independently wealthy enough to work on whatever subjects interested him most and to fund his own research. As Logan recalled, he was rather infamous for his skepticism of traditional scientific beliefs.

"One moment," Pace said. Sudden recognition had flashed in those calflike brown eyes. "Did you say your name was Logan?"

"That's right."

"Dr. Jeremy Logan?"

"Right again."

Pace took a deep breath. "Dr. Logan, excuse me for saying so, but I don't think I should be talking to you anymore about our lab. In fact, I shouldn't even have allowed you in. That's up to Laura to decide."

"Laura?" Logan asked.

At that moment, the door to the building opened and a woman stood framed in the entrance—tall, about thirty, with hazel eyes and high cheekbones: the woman in the photograph. She was wearing a Barbour jacket, and the wind had tousled her blond hair across her face and shoulders.

She looked from one man to the other. "I'm Laura Feverbridge," she told Logan in a musical contralto. "May I help you?"

"This is Jeremy Logan," Pace said. He hesitated a moment. "I, ah, I'm going to open those packages that arrived yesterday and store them in the equipment shed."

And with that he stepped out of the lab, leaving Logan with a woman he assumed was Dr. Feverbridge's daughter.

"What can I do for you, Mr. Logan?" Laura Feverbridge asked.

"First, let me say how sorry I am for the loss of your coworker. And no, I'm not in any way affiliated with the police."

Laura Feverbridge nodded. Logan took a step closer to her. He sensed uncertainty; shock; cautiousness; and deep, abiding sadness.

"I'll be frank with you. There are people here in the Adirondacks who think the three recent deaths—including that of your assistant, Artowsky—are not only tragic, but highly unusual. I've been asked, in an unofficial capacity, to look into them. I know this is probably not a good moment for you, but I wonder if you could spare just a few minutes of your time—and that of your father's as well, if it isn't asking too much."

As Logan spoke, the woman's eyes first widened, then narrowed again. "My father is dead."

"Oh," Logan replied, shocked. "I'm so sorry. I hadn't heard."

Laura Feverbridge hesitated for a moment. She blinked, drew the hair away from her eyes with one finger. Then she nodded toward the door. "Come on," she said. "We can talk out there."

14

They sat on rough wooden benches set parallel to the front door of the lab. Laura Feverbridge looked off into the woods, her hands clenched together.

"Again, I'm sorry to hear of your father's passing," Logan said. "The world has lost a brilliant naturalist."

"Actually, he held doctorates in both biochemistry and the natural sciences, and when he was younger lectured on both disciplines. But you're right—naturalism was always his first love."

This was followed by a short silence.

"What can you tell me about Artowsky?" Logan asked.

"I've already told the police just about everything," she said. "Mark was the most dedicated graduate student and lab assistant you could want. He was friendly, knowledgeable, interested in our work."

"His body was found about six miles north of here. Do you know how he happened to be so far from the lab?"

"Mark was a city boy his entire life. Queens born and bred. We were worried how he'd adapt to such a remote and isolated location. But ironically, he took to it with relish. Almost too much relish. He developed a love of hiking, but he wasn't very good at directions or orienteering. Twice he wandered off down unmarked trails and got lost overnight. Had to be rescued by rangers." At this, Laura Feverbridge managed a wintry smile.

"Did he have any enemies?"

"No. No enemies, no scientific rivals—certainly nobody here."

"Had he struck up relationships with any of the locals?"

"None of us have. We go into Saranac Lake twice a month to stock up on supplies and pick up packages at the post office. Otherwise, we keep to ourselves."

"If you had to guess what happened to Artowsky, what would you say?"

"That he'd wandered off again—and this time, ended up in the wrong place at the wrong time. They say it was the work of a bear—or maybe a feral wolf." She shuddered at the thought. "How horrible."

"Yes, it was. Horrible—and tragic." Logan paused. "Dr. Feverbridge, have you ever been to Pike Hollow?"

"No."

"Ever heard of a family called the Blakeneys?"

"No. These sound an awful lot like the questions the police asked. Are you sure you're not affiliated with them?"

"Quite the opposite. To be honest, Dr. Feverbridge, they wouldn't want me poking around like this."

"Then why are you?"

"It's like I said. There are members of the Adirondack community—responsible members—who have questions, *reservations,* about the nature of the deaths of the two backpackers, killed in a remote region several miles from here. I'm afraid that their reservations will extend to the death of Mr. Artowsky, as well."

"And just why did they ask you to look into it?"

"Let's say that my job is to examine things that lie beyond the scope of normal investigations—police or otherwise."

Laura Feverbridge did not respond to this. Instead, still looking off toward the woods, she gave a low whistle. Almost immediately, two Weimaraners, sleek and muscular, appeared from behind an outbuilding. They capered in front of the scientist, panting and whining, until she picked up a stick and threw it out toward the edge of the clearing. The two ran after it, barking excitedly.

"Beautiful dogs," Logan said.

"Thanks. Toshi and Mischa. They're almost like my own children."

"I have to ask. This is an unusual setting for a lab like yours—to say the least. From what I understand, your father had the wherewithal to do his research anyplace he liked. Why did you decide to come to such a remote location, which clearly comes with its own unique set of hardships?"

For a long moment, she did not respond. It was clear to Logan that she did not enjoy answering these questions. He also sensed something inside her—something going on beyond, or beneath, the ordinary. What it was, he couldn't tell. Nevertheless, she

seemed to be so dazed by the loss of Artowsky that she was operating on autopilot, answering the questions as they came without
thought. "You know of my father's work?"

"I know of his reputation, yes."

"Then you may or may not know that over the last few years
in particular he'd been subjected to increasingly withering scorn,
even derision, by the orthodox scientific community. Academics
can be an unforgiving, hateful lot, Mr. Logan. Schadenfreude,
or an embarrassing bit of peer review, seems never to be very far
away."

"I know. And it's Dr. Logan, actually. I teach history at Yale."

"Then you'll understand what I'm talking about. His theories
were ridiculed, articles called his work unscientific, even pseudoscience. My father was an honorable man, Dr. Logan. He took
great pride in his research. He tried to shrug it all off, but the
continued criticism wounded him deeply. At last, he went into a
kind of disgusted seclusion, determined not to be heard from pub-
licly again until his work was complete. And yet even that was not
enough—he grew so despondent that a time came when I truly
feared for him. And so I arranged for us to come out here—just
Father, myself, and our two graduate students—to continue his
research in a place where academic bitterness would have a hard
time reaching him."

"So what, exactly, was your father researching?" Logan
asked. "I know he was a naturalist, but beyond that very little."

A look of defensiveness came immediately over the woman's
face.

"Don't worry," Logan said. "You'll find that I'm the last person who would ever ridicule another scholar's theories."

"Because of your looking into things 'beyond the scope of the
normal,' you mean?"

"Exactly. My professional title—outside of Yale historian, that is—is enigmalogist."

She sighed. "Very well. I'm sure you'll understand if I don't go into detail. It had to do with something called the lunar effect."

"You mean, the correlation between the various stages of earth's lunar cycle and animal behavior?"

She looked at him in astonishment. "You've heard of it?"

"Given my avocation, are you surprised? Yes: it's the supposed connection between the full moon and the increased symptomology of epileptics, schizophrenics, and so forth."

"That's the simplistic view of it, anyway—and partly what gave my father such difficulties within the scientific community. And it is true there had been published studies on the 'lunar-lunacy connection': spikes in erratic behavior, suicides, psychiatric admissions, even increased traffic accidents and dog bites during certain phases of the moon. But I'm afraid our work here was much less sensational. I can't tell you everything. But part of my father's work involved mapping, very carefully and fully, the correlation of the lunar effect between nocturnal and diurnal animals. Small animals: shrews, bats. And as it turned out, this remote spot in the Adirondacks was ideal for both experimentation and observation. Now I'm determined to finish up the work he never got a chance to complete."

It was ironic, Logan thought, that Jessup's theories and Dr. Feverbridge's research both dealt, in very different ways, with the same thing: the moon. He wondered what Jessup knew, if anything, about Feverbridge's work. "How did he happen to die, if you don't mind my asking?"

"He was out hiking about six months ago. He liked the outdoors so—I think that's where Mark got his own taste for tramping around the forest. He was at the top of Madder's Gorge, a high point of land not two miles from here. He must have slipped, because he fell to the base of a waterfall, a few hundred feet below."

"How awful."

"I had to identify what was left of my poor father. It was . . . it was the hardest thing I've ever had to do. . . ." And here she fell silent.

Logan let the silence lengthen. He admired the courage of this woman, her evident determination, and her willingness to open up to a stranger about such a painful subject. The dogs returned, one with the stick in its mouth. It dropped it at Laura Feverbridge's feet, panting eagerly, and she picked it up and tossed it toward the woods once again.

"Anyway, continuing Father's research seemed the best way to honor his memory." She stood up. "And now, Dr. Logan, I think I'd better get back to it."

Logan stood up as well. "Of course. And I think you're brave to do so. Believe me, I know what it's like to have to work, knowing the entire world might be laughing at you. You've been very patient in answering my questions. I hope you'll forgive me if I ask just one more—and believe me when I say I don't mean to cause you any pain by it. You said you brought your father out to this remote place because you feared the academic scorn he'd been unrelentingly subjected to might make him . . . well, deeply depressed, at the very least. Can you be sure that his fall from the cliff wasn't intentional on his part?"

At this, the woman's hazel eyes clouded over. "No," she said after a long moment. "I've asked myself that, and there's no way I can ever be sure. I can only tell you that the seclusion brought him relief from the outside world—a place where the quiet could marshal his thoughts. He seemed happier to me here, more at peace with himself, than he had in years."

"Thank you, Dr. Feverbridge. I appreciate your candor. And I wish you the best of luck in completing your research."

"A pleasure to meet you, Dr. Logan."

They shook hands. Laura Feverbridge turned and disappeared into the laboratory, and Logan walked back to his Jeep.

He drove the hour-long trip back to Cloudwater deep in thought.

15

The following day began sunny and crisp, but by afternoon clouds had gathered and a fine mist was falling. After lunch, Logan bundled his laptop and notepad into his duffel, slung it over his shoulder, and made his way out of his cabin, along the network of paths, across the lawn, and into the great lodge. The receptionist nodded as he passed. All was quiet; he could almost imagine a great creative hive around him, busily working as—in countless private rooms—theses were being proposed, novels narrated, abstruse geometric theorems proven.

As was his nature, he had already explored the lodge and even some of its extensive grounds: he always felt more comfortable having a working knowledge of his surroundings. Now he made his way to the third floor and down its plushly carpeted hall to the heart of the building, where a half-open door revealed a narrow wooden stairway leading upward. He climbed it to a tiny room, nestled beneath the very eaves. This room, he'd learned, was known as "Forsythe's aerie." Back in the late nineteenth century, when Cloudwater had still been known as Rainshadow Lodge, the "Great Camp" had been the summer home of Willis J. Forsythe, a shipping magnate. He had, the story went, fancied himself something of an essayist and writer of belles lettres, and it had been his wont to come up to this tiny, uppermost room, where he could be certain of no distractions, in order to concentrate on writing. If the tactic had worked, Logan found no evidence of it: there were no books by Forsythe in Cloudwater's library.

The room was plain to the point of monasticism, containing only a single table and straight-backed wooden chair. It was empty, as he'd expected it would be. A single double-sashed window looked over the lawn and down to the mist-shrouded lake, and it was precisely this expansive view that he had come for: sitting in the Thomas Cole cabin that morning, he'd begun to feel hemmed in by trees, and he wanted a larger view in which to make the decision he realized now had to be made.

He took his laptop and notebook from the duffel and placed them on the table, though he doubted he'd need to refer to either one. Then he walked past the table and, hands behind his back, gazed out the window at the view below.

"Okay, Kit," he murmured to his dead wife. "Let's run it all up the flagpole, shall we?"

It was time to make a final effort to reevaluate everything he'd heard, read, and observed—if for no other reason than to fulfill his promise to his friend Randall Jessup.

First and foremost, there were the three murders. Each had occurred during a full moon; each had been perpetrated with extreme violence; and in each case it was uncertain who or what had done the killing. The third body, that of Artowsky, had been found some distance from the other two, but that in itself meant nothing except an extension of the kill zone. It was reasonable to assume the same being was responsible for all three deaths. A rogue bear had been the first opinion; most recently, the official theory was a wolf, although Captain Krenshaw leaned more toward a human killer, despite the remarkable strength required to tear bodies apart so violently.

The inhabitants of Pike Hollow, the closest hamlet to the murder sites, held the Blakeney clan responsible. The local belief—a belief of long standing—was that the Blakeneys were lycanthropes. Werewolves. He hadn't heard this from their own lips; he'd heard it from Jessup.

In the Saranac Lake library, he'd combed through the local newspapers going back fifty years. True, he'd come across a number of intriguing articles, sometimes splashed across the front pages, other times buried deep within: stories of strange sightings, maulings by animals, even the rare disappearance of a hunter or fisherman—not to mention the four young children who had vanished over the last two decades. None of these disappearances had been successfully accounted for, and no mention of the Blakeneys was made in the articles.

It was understandable that Jessup might suspect something unusual at work here, and Logan would be remiss not to keep in mind that his friend knew the locale far better than he did. On the other hand, he'd undertaken a dozen similar investigations, all over the world, and on every occasion he'd heard strange rumors, often sinister, always dark. Very rarely, they turned out to be true. And then, there was the other thing—despite his job as an enigmalogist, where keeping an open mind was essential to the game, something about the very notion of lycanthropy stuck in his craw. Not only that, but the Blakeneys—although he'd been personally threatened by them—seemed too much of an obvious scapegoat.

The readings of the air ion counter, EM detector, and other equipment he'd tested at a variety of sites were all inconclusive. That left only one item to consider: the unsettling feelings that, as a sensitive, he'd been aware of every time he drove down the forest-haunted 3A into deeper and deeper wilderness ... wilderness he'd never experienced, or even known to exist, on his weekend trips to the High Peaks as a younger man. He could come to only one conclusion: the Adirondacks itself was full of an unplumbed, untamable force of nature that was—while not malignant, exactly—at best indifferent to man and, at worst, inimical. It was an irresistibly strong force that overwhelmed his ability as an empath to make specific observations or to absorb particular feelings, beyond the general sense that something was amiss; alien.

And that, he realized, made him useless to his friend the ranger.

Still looking out the window, he pulled out his cell phone, checked to make sure it had reception—a habit he'd developed since arriving—and made a call.

"Jessup here," the voice on the other end answered.

"It's Jeremy."

"Jeremy, hi. Anything new to report?"

"Nothing. Except that I've done a lot of thinking, and ... well, I've decided to throw in the towel."

There was silence on the other end of the line.

"Look, Randall. I've done all I can to help. I've talked to the locals, investigated the deaths, even viewed the third one with my own eyes. I've tried for your sake to keep an open mind. I've spent ten times as many hours on this as I'd originally agreed to. But I've run up against a brick wall."

"What about the Blakeneys?"

"Krenshaw is already keeping a close eye on them, as you know. The plain fact is, I'm not finding any leads. I simply haven't come across a shred of evidence, hard or soft, to justify my looking into things further. I hate to say it, but the time has come to let law enforcement—you included—do its job. And the fact is I'm losing precious ground on the project I came here to complete. I also think that Hartshorn, the resident director, is getting suspicious of my comings and goings. He gave me a look as I went into dinner last night that I didn't care for. I don't want to be summarily given the heave-ho from Cloudwater." He paused. "I'm sorry. I know you feel strongly about this, and I wish I had something more positive to say. But without any measurable progress, I just can't afford to give it any more time."

It took Jessup a moment to answer. "I understand. And I appreciate it—I really do. You've gone out of your way to help, which was more than I had reason to expect, appearing on your doorstep like I did after being out of touch for so long."

"Don't think twice about that."

Another pause. "But Jeremy . . . before you abandon this and go back to your research full-time, would you do me one last favor?"

"What is it?" Logan asked guardedly.

"Would you take a trip out with me tomorrow morning to speak with Saul Woden?"

"Saul Woden?" Logan repeated. The name sounded familiar— and then he remembered where he'd heard it: from Krenshaw, during the briefing at the ranger station. *This wasn't the work of an animal, and it sure as hell wasn't the work of a monster. In fact, I've got a pretty good idea who's responsible.*

"I've had a chance to look into this Woden," Jessup said. "Turns out he savagely murdered two people twenty-five years before—down in the Catskills, not around here—was found not guilty by reason of insanity, and was sentenced to the mental institution outside Schoharie. He was paroled a year ago. The state declared him rehabilitated. Now he lives alone outside Big Moose, a hamlet about forty miles away from you, on the edge of the Raven Lake Wilderness."

"What good would my talking to him do?" Logan said, but even as he asked the question he guessed the answer.

"Because . . . I want to know your take on the man. Could he possibly be our killer? Can I get behind Krenshaw and his official suspicion? I just need to know I can put this gut feeling of mine aside, once and for all."

Logan sighed. He'd done so much already—he might as well do this one last thing. "Very well. But you understand that, after this, I'm done. I've got a date with the Middle Ages."

"Fair enough."

"Can you meet me out at the main entrance again? And can you make it early, say before breakfast? The last thing I need is to have Hartshorn see me heading out with you."

"I'll be there at six thirty."

"Okay. And Randall? Whether this fellow Woden is rehabilitated or not, you will be bringing your sidearm with you—right?"

"Wouldn't have it any other way. See you in the morning." And with that, the phone went dead.

16

"So what have you learned about this Saul Woden, exactly?" Logan asked at last. They had been driving for the past hour, and conversation had been sporadic. Jessup seemed on edge, and Logan could well understand: he, too, felt a sense of agitation, as if they were heading toward something best left alone, and already more than once he'd regretted agreeing to this visit.

"I reread the file last night," the ranger replied. "It's there between the seats if you want to take a look."

"I'd rather hear it from you."

"Woden grew up in a remote section of the Catskills. To say he was imperfectly socialized is putting it mildly. He was brutalized by his parents, especially his father, who left when Woden was about seven. The child had emotional problems that were mistaken for a learning disability—his mother apparently hated him for it and, once he reached puberty, no longer bothered trying to see to his education and, in fact, basically kicked him out of the house. He spent most of his time alone in the woods, where his condition worsened. Finally, when he was twenty, he killed two people with an ax—chopped them almost to bits. One was a young man, a backpacker, who happened across the little lean-to Woden had fashioned for himself. This happened during a full moon. The other was a girl of seventeen, who had a job at a Laundromat in a nearby village and was biking home after work. This was four days later, in the early evening, when the moon was waning. When caught—he didn't try to resist arrest—Woden raved about being persecuted, about the voices that whispered to him in the night, about the two he'd killed being 'dark saints' come to steal his soul."

"Delusions of persecution," Logan said. "Auditory hallucinations. Sounds like a paranoid schizophrenic."

"That was the conclusion of the state. He was found not guilty by reason of insanity and committed to a downstate institution. As I already told you, he was released on parole about a year ago. He was monitored carefully during the parole period and adjudged to be rehabilitated. That was when he moved out into the wilderness—six months ago."

And wilderness it was, Logan thought. From Tupper Lake, they had struck out southwest and, eventually, entered a kind of forest he had never experienced before. The trunks of the trees grew remarkably thick and gnarled, twisted and bent as if arthritic; what leaves remained on the skeletal branches were almost black in color. They were primarily deciduous, with only a few of the tall, stately, pleasantly scented pines that were so common around Cloudwater. Every now and then, a bog or lake could be seen between the trunks: brackish and sullen-looking, dark as the lowering trees that surrounded it. He saw no signs of habitation, and they passed only one vehicle—a decrepit Ford pickup, vintage 1950. The road was worse than even the ones he'd traveled over on the way to Pike Hollow, and Jessup's truck rattled and shook as if any moment it might fly apart.

"Where exactly are we?" Logan asked.

"Raven Lake Wilderness."

The cab of the truck fell into another extended silence.

"How is it that you didn't know of this man's coming into the region?" Logan asked at length. "I'd have thought that would come under the category of news."

"His prison time, his parole, all took place far to the south of here. When his parole term was up, he came north—quietly. It was as if he wanted to get as far away from people, and civilization, as possible. But as a felon, he had to register his current address with the parole board. I guess Krenshaw's downstate cronies must have alerted him. The state police knew, but we didn't. Don't forget—us rangers are spread pretty thin. There are only about a hundred of us to cover the entire state. We can't know everything, be everywhere."

"Speaking of being everywhere, how's the search coming?"

Jessup grimaced. "Terrible. We've called in rangers from four separate zones. And we've found nothing—no bears, no wolves, no clues. We'll be calling it off in a day or two—otherwise, I think we'd have a mutiny on our hands."

"I assume Krenshaw has spoken to Woden himself?"

"A couple of times. Apparently the interviews didn't go very well. He's still suspect number one. At this point, Krenshaw's just waiting him out, hoping he'll try something again."

Up ahead, in the distance, a state police vehicle became visible in the woven tangle of trees. "We must be close," Jessup said. "Get down onto the floor."

"Why?"

"Krenshaw's put a cordon around Woden's place. But not too close—he probably knows that would agitate the man. I'd rather not have Krenshaw find out I've brought you here."

Logan did as requested. He felt the truck creep forward, then stop.

"Morning, Officer," he heard Jessup say.

"Lieutenant," came the clipped reply from outside and below.

"How far ahead is he?"

"Quarter mile. Just around the bend."

"The captain has one or two questions she wants me to put to Woden. Don't worry, nothing that will alarm him. I'll only be a few minutes. Will you keep a watch here? I'll let you know if I need you."

"Will do."

"Thanks." And with that the truck eased forward again. As Logan crouched on the floor, the jouncing of the vehicle was even more pronounced. He felt the truck go around a bend, hit a particularly deep rut, then come to a halt.

"We're here," Jessup said. "You can get out."

Logan eased himself up, then opened the door and stepped out. At first, he saw nothing but a veritable whirlwind of trees, shrubs, and bracken surrounding the vehicle. And then he made out, against the riot of brown and black, a cavelike hut, its interior seemingly pulled by hand out of the all-encompassing blowdowns, the way a rodent might pull moss and verdure from a hollow tree stump in order to make a nest. A single low wall of rotting, unpainted two-by-fours made up both a facade and a prop against the collapse of the broken limbs that formed the ceiling. Beyond the truck, Logan could see the "road"—barely a grassy path at this point—curving away into the dimness.

Jessup gave Logan a nod—of both caution and encouragement—checked his weapon, then moved forward. Logan followed.

Reaching the front door—sagging in its jambs, with leather thongs for hinges—Jessup raised a hand to knock. But Logan stopped him, stepped forward himself, and gave a single rap.

"Mr. Woden?" he asked. "Saul Woden?"

There was no response from inside.

"My name's Logan. Jeremy Logan. I'm not with the police. I just want five minutes of your time."

Still nothing.

"You see, Saul, I need help—and I think that maybe you can help me. Would you let me in for just a moment? Please?"

For a minute, there was no response. Then a rattling sounded from inside and the door opened a crack. Two eyes like glowing coals peered out from the darkness.

"I'm Jeremy," Logan repeated. "Could I come in for just a minute? I won't stay long, I promise."

The man hesitated. Then he opened the door wider. Logan stepped in, nodding deferentially as he did so. Jessup followed.

Saul Woden was short, but very powerfully built. He had a matted beard and hair that spilled down around his shoulders. His most prominent features were his eyes: bright, skittish. They widened in alarm when they saw the ranger enter. He was dressed in clothes that were old and worn nearly to tatters, but quite clean. The same could not be said for his dwelling: as his eyes adjusted to the dimness, Logan saw that a wattle-and-daub roof had been fashioned into the blowdown over their heads, and more two-by-fours had been used for walls to the left and right. A kerosene lamp hung from a wooden peg set into the ceiling, which grew lower toward the rear of the single room, until at the back one had to stoop to move around. There was a mattress, torn and frayed and without a blanket. An unpleasant odor lingered in the air. Along one wall, countless tins of food had been stacked almost to the ceiling. Two sawn stumps of wood, one larger than the other, made up the only things that could be considered furniture. It was like Jessup said: Woden had deliberately tried to remove himself from all semblance of civilization.

A number of bottles of clozapine—some empty, others not yet opened—lay scattered around the floor.

"What do you want?" Woden said. "I ain't done nothing."

"I know that," Logan said calmly. "Can we just sit for a minute?" And he indicated the stumps of wood.

"I ain't done nothing," Woden repeated. "Those police already been bothering me. I ain't done nothing!"

His voice had grown shrill during this short recitation, and the eyes wider, the whites bulging. Logan realized he had very little time to accomplish what they'd come for.

"I'm a researcher," he said in the same soothing tones. He took a seat on one of the rough stumps. "I investigate past events. I'm not here about any of those police matters."

He already sensed that he'd get nothing out of Woden regarding the recent killings, whether the man was responsible for them or not. All he could hope for was a reading of the man's psyche, a small window into his inner soul.

Now, slowly and suspiciously, Woden sat down on the other stump. His eyes darted nervously toward Jessup once or twice, who stood close to the doorway, arms at his sides, maintaining a nonthreatening posture, hands holding nothing more than his omnipresent notebook.

"Saul," Logan said, "I know what you did. But that was a

long time ago. And you're better now. You've been cured. You're taking medication. I'm not here to judge you. I'm just here to . . . to *understand*. I have a certain ability to do that, you see." He chose his words carefully, knowing Woden had suffered a persecution complex. "And maybe I can even help you. I just need a single favor. May I take hold of one of your hands?"

Woden jerked in surprise. His hands curled into fists.

"It helps me understand the person I'm speaking to. This way, I won't have to ask any questions, and you won't have to say a thing. Not a thing. I know it might sound strange, but trust me." And then, slowly, he held out one hand, palm open and upraised.

Logan's soothing, unmodulated voice, his slow gestures, had the effect he intended. Although he still looked nervous, Woden's fists relaxed. Slowly—as if approaching something very hot—he put one hand forward. Logan noticed that although the hand itself was clean, there was considerable dirt beneath the fingernails.

Logan took the hand gently between his own. "Now, Saul, I'm going to ask you one last favor—just one. And then I'll go, and I won't bother you again. I want you to think back—in your own way—on those bad things you did."

Woden's expression grew alarmed, and he tried to pull back his hand. But Logan restrained him, gently but firmly. "Just think back for a moment. What happened—and why."

Woden was looking at him. And suddenly, Logan was filled with a wave of emotion so powerful it almost pushed him off his chair. He was flooded with fear: there was nobody he could trust; everyone around him wished him harm; there was no rest, not even in sleep; and the voices would never leave him—those whispering voices that at times taunted him, at times warned him, at times commanded him. A psychological desolation, a kind of existential despair such as he'd never experienced, pierced Logan to the core. The voices grew louder, more insistent; as if from a great distance he saw an ax, became aware of its reassuring, comforting weight in his hands—there was sudden, involuntary action, a series of ragged screams, and then the voices swelled in jubilation before subsiding into silence. But all too quickly, they began their chanting murmur again—and the darkness once again rushed to embrace him. . . .

For the first time he could remember, Logan snatched his hand away in the midst of an empathetic encounter. Unwillingly, he looked at Woden. The man was staring back. The alarm had left his eyes, and instead there was a strange, almost intimate look in them, as if they had passed on a secret; as if a part of Woden was now part of Logan, and would never leave him.

Shakily, Logan got to his feet. "Thank you," he managed. "We'll leave you now."

He stumbled in the doorway, and Jessup helped him back into the truck, had him crouch once again until they had passed the state policeman. Then the ranger stopped the car, raised Logan into his seat, and strapped him in.

All the way back to Cloudwater, Jessup knew enough to say nothing, keeping quiet while Logan recovered and marshaled his thoughts. Just before the entrance to Cloudwater, he pulled the truck onto the shoulder and looked at his friend in mute inquiry.

Logan returned the look. "I'll tell you what I experienced," he said. "But only once. Please don't ask me to talk of it again. It will be hard enough to forget as it is."

Jessup nodded.

"I sensed overwhelming fear. I sensed a very sick mind. I sensed violence—savage violence. But that violence seemed . . . old to me. Still very much alive in his mind—but old."

"Could Woden have committed these three murders?" Jessup asked quietly.

"I don't know. I wouldn't rule it out. As I said, I didn't sense anything that felt recent—that he was killing in the present. But there was so much violence in his past there's no way for me to be sure. He may well have been rehabilitated, as the state says. Clearly they believe he's no longer capable of murder, or they wouldn't have paroled him. But *I* believe he's capable . . . and dangerous."

Jessup nodded again. Then he sighed. "Thank you, Jeremy— for everything, but especially for this. If I'd known how much of an ordeal it would be, I'd never have asked. Maybe Krenshaw's right, after all. In any case, that will be my assumption, going forward. Can I drive you in?"

"No, thanks. I'd rather walk, if it's all the same to you."

"Sure. I'll call you in a few days. We'll have you over for dinner again—and no shoptalk, I promise."

"Okay." And Logan got out of the truck, waited for it to disappear down the road, then began making his way down the lane to Cloudwater.

17

Logan walked slowly, trying to still the agitation and dismay that he felt. As a sensitive, he'd had numerous unpleasant encounters in the past—though few as disturbing as this one—and as he walked he employed a mental exercise: as calmly and rationally as he could, he went over the encounter one final time. And then, quite deliberately, he put it inside of a box, shut the box, and stored it away in a far corner of his mind where—hopefully—it would remain without troubling his dreams.

He turned in at the path to his cottage, glanced at his watch. To his surprise, it was almost a quarter to two. He felt utterly drained; there would be no work for him today. He passed the turnoff for the Albert Bierstadt cabin, the William Hart cabin, then took the final turn toward his own. As he did so, he stopped, frowning in surprise. Ahead, he could see that someone was sitting on his front steps. It was Pace, the technician he'd met the other day; the one who worked for Laura Feverbridge.

What on earth could he want? Logan wondered. Clearly, the man wasn't aware of Cloudwater's no-uninvited-visitors policy. This was the last thing he needed: his only desire at the moment was to go inside, pour himself a stiff drink despite the early hour, lie down on the couch, and close his eyes. But with an effort he put a spring into his step and approached the cabin. His lunch, he saw, had been left on its usual tray, beneath a pair of stainless-steel dish covers.

"Kevin Pace, right?" he said as the technician stood at his approach.

Pace nodded.

"Have you been waiting long?"

"About half an hour." The man passed a hand through his rumpled, mouse-colored hair. "I'm sorry to bother you. I remembered your saying you were in the Thomas Cole cabin, and I wandered the grounds until I found it." He seemed agitated, his eyes darting here and there even though the two of them were standing at the path's end, invisible to anyone. "I'm sorry, but do you think I could speak to you for a minute?"

"Of course." Careful to keep the puzzlement from his face, Logan unlocked the door, ushered the man in, then picked up the lunch tray and followed.

"Sit anywhere," he said as he carried the tray to the kitchen, then came back out into the living room. Pace sat down on the wraparound couch and Logan chose a chair opposite him. The technician licked his lips, wiped his hands on his jeans. It did not take an empath to see that he was upset about something, perhaps even frightened.

"Why don't you tell me what I can do for you," Logan said, leaning forward, interlacing his fingers and resting them on his knees.

But even though he'd driven all the way from the research station, even though he'd waited on Logan's step for thirty minutes, the technician seemed unwilling to talk—or, perhaps more likely, didn't know how to begin. He cleared his throat, looked at Logan with his timid eyes, took a deep breath.

"It's okay," Logan said. "Whatever it is, I'm sure I've heard stranger."

Pace took another deep breath. "How much did Dr. Feverbridge tell you about our work?"

"She said you've been studying the influence of the lunar effect on small mammals."

Pace nodded slowly. "Yes. It's been taking longer than expected—everything slowed down, of course, after her father died. Anyway, my own observations have dealt mainly with *Peromyscus maniculatus* and *Blarina brevicauda*."

"Excuse me?"

"Oh. Sorry." And for the first time in Logan's brief experience, Pace smiled. "The deer mouse and the northern short-tailed shrew. I was assigned the shrew specifically because of the morphological changes they go through during torpor—their teeth, skulls, even internal organs undergo significant shrinkage. Among other things, I've been tasked with determining if those changes can be stimulated in ways other than weather."

"Go on," Logan said.

"Well, as you might imagine, because I study the rodents— well, technically, a shrew isn't a rodent—at various phases of the moon, my work involves observations both inside the laboratory and out, at night as well as day."

Logan nodded. It was as if Pace was dancing around the issue, unwilling to get to the point.

"I do most of my nightly observations in 'A Pen'—that's a

small blind we attached to the rear of the main lab. The fact is . . . well, I've started to hear things."

"Things?"

"Strange noises in the night. Mutterings, whisperings, the occasional muffled bang. I don't much like being so deep out in the woods—unlike Mark Artowsky, who took to it like a fish to water—and at first I just chalked it up to an overactive imagination. But then I saw the lights."

"Where?"

"Hard to tell, with all the trees. But they seemed to come from the direction of an old outbuilding."

"An outbuilding of the fire station?"

Pace nodded. "We've never used it. It's situated too deep in the woods, out south behind the lab."

"When did you first notice this?" Logan asked.

The technician thought a moment. "Hard to be sure. I think it was around the time that second backpacker's body was discovered. But it may have been earlier." He hesitated. "I tried not to think about it, tried to blame it on cabin fever. And maybe that's what it is. But after what happened to Mark . . . I just needed to tell somebody about it. I couldn't keep it to myself any longer."

"Why didn't you mention this to the police?" Logan asked. It was a fair enough question: the cops had already been out to interview the lab personnel after the discovery of Artowsky's body.

"I wanted to, believe me. But a story as thin as this? I figured they'd think I was crazy. And if they didn't, then they'd be swarming all over the lab, interfering with our work more than they already have, and . . . and asking more questions." At the thought, Pace seemed to grow more agitated. "And that's the last thing I want. I don't want to get any more involved."

All of a sudden, he looked directly at Logan. "But then *you* stopped by the lab. Scientific curiosity, you said—and a wish to express your condolences. Those were the reasons for your visit. But I know who you are. I saw you interviewed in that PBS documentary about Bigfoot. I guessed the real reason you stopped by our lab . . . and after thinking about it, I realized you were the perfect person to tell."

Logan didn't respond. *Serves me right,* he thought ruefully.

Pace glanced down at his hands. "It's just that I know bad stuff has been happening, out there in the western wilderness. And since I'd been hearing some strange things, seeing things . . . and since I know a little about your work—well, I figured you'd be more receptive than a cop, or a ranger. That's all."

For a moment, Logan didn't reply. Then he nodded. "Okay."

"So what are you going to do?" Pace asked.

"Do? Well, right now, I'm going to take a long nap." And he stood up. "Thanks for coming by. I know this doesn't come naturally to you, getting something like this off your chest. But I hope you'll feel better for having done so." He smiled and offered the technician his hand.

Pace blinked for a moment, not comprehending. Then, all of a sudden, he scrambled to his feet, shook the proffered hand.

"Thanks," he said. Then a fresh look of anxiety swept over his face as a new thought came to him. "You won't tell the police you heard anything from me?"

"Heard what? This conversation never took place."

Pace nodded as Logan led him to the door.

"Drive carefully. And good luck with your research."

Pace blinked, nodded again. Then he turned and began hurrying back down the path to the parking lot.

18

All the next day, and the day following, Logan worked assiduously on his monograph. Except that, try as he might, he was not able to make much headway. He wasted hours verifying sources he'd already confirmed to his satisfaction; he reread passages he had previously polished and left for done. He spent altogether too much time staring out the window at the surrounding trees, wondering how much progress was being made in the cottages around him: Diane Kearns, the conceptual artist, toiling at "Works in Progress Nos. 74 & 75"; Rudolph Zeiss writing his single-movement concerto for piano and string orchestra.

Gradually, he became aware of the cause of this distractedness: it was Kevin Pace, and his talk of lights and strange noises in the woods behind the fire station. As much as Logan had told himself—and Jessup—that he was finished inquiring into the murders, and as much as he wanted to believe it, he realized that he'd already put so much time and thought into the investigation that he wouldn't be able to rest until he had looked into this, too. It might be nothing, it was almost certainly nothing . . . and yet the coincidence—unexplained goings-on near the lab where the most recent victim had worked, not far from Desolation Mountain—was something his sixth sense told him simply could not be ignored.

And so, after dinner that second day, he got into his rented Jeep and left Cloudwater, heading west on Route 3 toward Pike Hollow. As unattractive as the prospect of driving into the deep woods after dark was, Pace had said he'd heard the noises only at night. Besides, Logan had had little enough reason to visit the fire station the first time—he could think of no excuse to show up by daylight a second time and go poking about. He wouldn't be trespassing, exactly; no doubt the Feverbridges had leased or rented the building from the state. He'd take a look around, satisfy himself that nothing was amiss, and leave. And maybe then he'd be able to get on with his work.

The woods were dark and close enough when driving through during the day; at night, it felt like he was burrowing into an endless, living thicket. He was surrounded by a blackness that was unnerving in its totality. Not a single car passed by heading east; it was as if he were alone on a planet tenanted only by trees. As he drove, he was careful to keep his mind away from Saul Woden and the terrifying, writhing violence he'd sensed within the man. Instead, he tried to think about Pace. He tried to tell himself this was a fool's errand—he was wasting his time on a young man's imagination, spooked by the deep woods and the recent murders. And yet his thoughts kept returning to the one question that had been left unasked in his conversation with Pace, the question that was at least in part responsible for prompting this nocturnal enterprise: *Why didn't you report what you'd heard to Laura Feverbridge?*

He found the intersection with 3A, passed the turnoffs for Pike Hollow and the Blakeney compound, and then—slowing to a crawl—navigated the forks in the narrow dirt track beyond that left the highway and led still deeper into the woods. This time, to his great relief, he managed to avoid getting lost—the route was still fresh in his memory—and in short order he could make out faint lights through the fretted trunkwork of forest. Immediately, he killed his own headlights, stopped the Jeep, and turned off the engine. He sat for a minute, listening to the ticking of the engine as it cooled. Then he picked up a handheld GPS navigator and lithium-powered flashlight from the passenger's seat, opened the door, slipped out, and shut the door as quietly as he could behind him.

He stood in the darkness a minute, breathing in the night air. Through the network of branches overhead, a pale moon was just visible behind dark, swollen clouds. There was a rumble of thunder. He was vaguely aware of a sense that something was *wrong* somehow; of a kind of violation of the natural order of things. But this was something he always sensed out here, beyond Pike Hollow, close to the Five Ponds Wilderness—and the Blakeney residence.

His eight-thousand-candlepower flashlight was exceptionally bright, and he dialed it back to its lowest setting. He aimed it at the ground, switched it on just long enough to establish his bearings and get a sense of the dirt lane ahead of him. He glanced at his watch: ten thirty. And then, with a deep breath, he set forward. In the distance ahead, he could hear the barking and whining of dogs. The night breeze was blowing into his face; it couldn't be his presence that had disturbed them. He hoped they were not roaming free; if they were, his little nocturnal escapade might end prematurely.

Slowly, as he walked on—using the flashlight now and then to orient himself—the faint lights of the lab became sharper. And then he stepped into the clearing. The collapsed fire tower itself was like a severed black finger stabbing skyward. The main laboratory building was dark, the generator rumbling quietly beyond it. The lights he had been following came, he now saw, from a building on the far side of the parking area; evidently, this was the living quarters. As he watched, a figure moved behind a curtained window.

He hesitated a second, considering how best to proceed. Then he began walking in a semicircle along the edge of the clearing, sticking close to the wall of trees, staying far from the living quarters. He passed the fire tower and the lab, passed a few small outbuildings—dark and, for the most part, shuttered and in disrepair. The moon, fully obscured now by clouds, shed only the faintest of light, and he was forced to use the torch more frequently as he made his way through grass and knee-high saplings.

Five minutes brought him to the far side of the clearing. From here, he could see what looked like a naturalist's blind—a structure he assumed to be Pace's "A Pen"; a storage depot; and across the clearing, a large run of chain link that, to his great relief, housed the two dogs. He could just make out their dark figures, running back and forth and whimpering. They were ignoring him entirely, facing away, evidently distracted in the opposite direction.

He paused once again to reconnoiter. Pace had said the lights and noises had come from an old outbuilding deep in the woods, south of the lab. He moved carefully along the southern fringe of trees, then stopped when the moon came out briefly from behind the clouds. The faintest of tracks could be seen here, heading south from the clearing into the forest. The living quarters were now obscured by outbuildings, and he ventured to use the flashlight again, tracing the path as it meandered between the trees. There was no sound save for the whisper of wind in the branches, the distant generator, and the worrying noises of the dogs.

. . . But wait: was that a faint flickering of light ahead, far into the trees? Wasn't that a low susurrus of voices: first one speaking, then another?

He began making his way along the narrow path, using the flashlight still more frequently now that he was out of the clearing and in amid the dense woods. There it was again: a low voice, followed by another.

Abruptly, the wind shifted and the whining of the dogs became a sudden, frantic racket: they had caught his scent. *Damn.* He moved more quickly along the path, hoping to get out of range, but the chorus of loud barking continued for several minutes before eventually dying away. When it did, he paused to listen. Nothing now: no voices, just the faint night sounds of the woods. Had he heard them at all, or was it his—and Pace's—imagination?

It was utterly dark ahead, no lights whatsoever, and now Logan used his flashlight continuously to guide him along the narrow, twisting trail. Another minute, and a building loomed out of the woods ahead: a long, low, dilapidated structure with a metal roof and perhaps half a dozen windows, all covered by what looked like heavy, rotting burlap. It sat in the middle of a tiny clearing. What the structure's original purpose might have been—dormitory, mess—or why it was situated out here in the middle of the forest, he couldn't imagine. What was clear was that it looked dark and untenanted.

He played his light slowly over the structure, from one end to the other. Was this the source of the lights and noises Pace claimed to have heard? It seemed likely: the narrow trail ended here, at the building's sole door.

Logan hesitated a moment, but there was nothing save the distant whining of the dogs. He approached the door, grasped the old-fashioned handle.

It was unlocked. He depressed the plunger with his thumb, eased the door open, and stepped inside. Then, closing the door behind him, he began a circuit of the interior with his flashlight.

What he saw was a revelation. Instead of the clutter and debris he was expecting—old tables and benches, covered with cobwebs and mice droppings—the ramshackle building contained a small laboratory. It appeared to have been rather hastily assembled but was nevertheless, if anything, even more modern than the one in which Laura Feverbridge and Pace worked. The beam of his torch licked over an autoclave; a centrifuge; two types of compound microscopes; a mass spectrometer; a UV transilluminator; what looked like a capillary gel DNA sequencer; and a host of other instruments Logan did not recognize. A door in the far wall led to another room, within which he could make out a narrow cot. As in the main lab, there were several cages for small animals— mice, moths, caterpillars, salamanders—set on wooden shelving. A very large, drum-shaped lamp with a grilled front lens, of the kind used in photography and film studios, hung from a wheeled stand, and there was other optical equipment scattered about as well. Nevertheless, on the whole the research equipment here seemed more medical in nature than that in the primary lab.

Suddenly, Logan froze. The beam of his flashlight stopped, in its transit of the room, on two figures, standing silent and motionless in a corner. One of them was Laura Feverbridge. She was holding a shotgun, and it was pointed at Logan. The other was an elderly man, very tall and gaunt, with a heavy salt-and-pepper beard and a shock of white hair—the man Logan had seen in the photo on the lab table.

Chase Feverbridge. Laura's father—who had fallen to his death while hiking six months before.

19

For a moment, all three of them stood as if frozen. Then, slowly, Laura Feverbridge lowered the shotgun.

"Would you mind taking that light out of our eyes, Dr. Logan?" she asked.

Logan aimed the light away. There was another rumble of distant thunder outside.

Now Logan understood: the sudden barking of the dogs had alerted the two, and they had turned out the lights in hopes of not being discovered. But that was the only thing he did understand. Nothing else about this situation made any sense.

The elderly man looked at Logan through the indirect glow of the flashlight, his expression a mixture of confusion, surprise, and something else. "You know this man, Laura?" he asked. His voice was deep and resonant, with the faintest touch of an English accent.

"Jeremy Logan. He visited the lab a few days ago."

"Well, you might as well turn on the lights," the man continued. "No point chatting in the dark."

She looked at him questioningly. "Father?"

"Why not? If he'd brought the cavalry with him, they'd be here by now."

After a moment, Laura Feverbridge reached over and flicked a switch. An overhead light came on, illuminating the lab.

She smiled a little wanly at Logan. "After you left, Kevin told me about the unusual nature of your work. I wondered if our paths might cross again. But I didn't expect it would be here."

Logan nodded at the shotgun. "What's that for?"

"You're kidding, right? After what happened to Mark?"

"Fair enough. But this *is* your father—correct?" Logan turned to the man. "You're Chase Feverbridge?"

The elderly man did not reply for a moment. Then he nodded slowly. His eyes were a piercing blue, and they seemed to see right through Logan. "If you don't mind," he said, "I'm going to sit down." And he walked over to a nearby worktable, took a seat on a lab stool.

Laura hesitated a moment, then seemed to come to a decision. "I guess I'd better explain all this to you," she said. "In fact, it looks like I don't have a choice. It's either that . . . or shoot you."

"I'd rather it was the former," Logan said.

At this, the older man gave a ghost of a smile. "Laura," he said, "under the circumstances, don't you think it would be better if I—"

"No, Father. Let me do it." She drew in a deep, shuddering

breath. Then, using the muzzle of the shotgun, she motioned Logan to follow her out of the building.

They emerged into the cool night. Laura closed the door softly behind them as Logan turned off his flashlight. She took a few steps away, toward the edge of the small clearing, and he followed. No sound came from the main camp, and Logan could see no lights through the trees.

There was a sudden spike in the distant whining and yowling of the dogs. "What's with them?" he asked.

"Toshi and Mischa? I've begun keeping them in that run at night—if there is a rogue bear or wolf on the loose, I don't want them to encounter it. And the truth is they've been acting strangely—as if some unfamiliar animal is nearby in the woods. That's the only reason I can think of for the way they've taken up snarling and whimpering after dark."

She stood in the wash of obscured moonlight, shotgun cradled in her arms, collecting her thoughts. Then she looked straight at Logan, her expression determined, even defiant. "Look. I've already told you why we established our lab here. Not only is it an ideal place for our research, but it helped shield my father from the relentless criticism his work had been subjected to. And all that was true. But it wasn't enough. Even here, the criticism reached us—by Internet and e-mail. My father is a very proud man . . . but he's also troubled, vulnerable. Despite his brilliance, he's always been emotionally fragile. After our arrival, he continued to grow increasingly distraught. 'Deterioration' might be a better word. I know you can understand, Dr. Logan, because I imagine you've had a taste of it yourself—it's one thing to face rejection, but quite another to be an object of scorn, even condemnation, from those who should be your peers. And then, he published those last two articles . . . but he did it prematurely, submitted without my knowledge, promising much in the text but without the necessary scientific underpinnings and relevant data. I guess he was lashing out at his detractors, trying to prove his point. The result was precisely the opposite he'd hoped for—he was subjected to academic ridicule even more severe. It was then that he . . . tried to kill himself."

"What?" Logan said. "Here?"

She nodded. "I came into the dormitory just as he was about to hang himself. Another five minutes, and I'd have been too late. As I was cutting the rope, he told me not to bother; he'd just find some other way to take his life."

She chewed her lip. "I didn't know what else I could do. I'd brought us to this utterly remote place—and yet even that wasn't enough. I felt helpless. I went out one day for a walk, down one of Mark's favorite paths. I needed to get away from the lab, try to think, try to figure out what to do. And that's when it happened. About two miles from the lab, I came upon a body—a human body. It lay at the bottom of Madder's Gorge, at the base of the waterfall. It was a man, maybe sixty or seventy. . . . I couldn't tell for certain, he was too broken up and bloodied. It must have just happened. It was awful." She shuddered at the memory. "What was clear was that he'd fallen from a height of land overhead. There were rocks strewn around him, and I could see the spot above where the cliff face had given way. I was horrified, about to turn and run for the authorities—but for some reason I didn't. See, an idea came to me, I don't know from where. But all of a sudden, I thought that maybe—just maybe—I'd found the answer I was looking for."

She took another deep breath. "Near the body was a back-pack. I rifled through it. It contained what you'd expect—food, cooking equipment, sleeping bag . . . and a diary. I paged quickly through that diary. It turned out the corpse was that of a survivalist, a nomad. He'd been living off the grid for years. The journal was a sort of confessional; a catalog of his personal convictions, his charges against civilization. This was a man with no relations to speak of, certainly none that he cared for or that cared for him; a man who had unplugged himself from the world, turned his back on everything he'd known, and spent years roaming the North American wilderness, letting whim guide his feet, bedding down where he pleased."

She fell silent. The silence stretched on so long Logan realized he'd better continue the story for her.

"In short, a man nobody would miss," he said.

She nodded. "He was about my father's height, and build, and age. Beyond that, he was . . . unrecognizable. It was like a gift. A strange and terrible gift. I'd walked out, looking for an answer—and here one lay, literally at my feet. I ran back to the camp. It took some convincing, but eventually my father agreed—especially when I explained that this was the best way, the *only* way, to free him once and for all. I took my father's wallet, ran back to the waterfall, and exchanged it for the dead man's few pitiful papers. I retrieved the backpack and buried it out in the woods behind the lab. I burned the journal. I installed my father here, in this remote outbuilding, where nobody would bother him or discover him. And the next day, I reported to the authorities that he was missing. I knew it wouldn't be long before somebody found the body—a cop, or a ranger, or Mark on one of his hikes. And that was exactly what happened. Naturally, when they found my father's wallet they asked me to identify the mutilated body. I did—at least, I said I did. A week later, they returned his ashes to me. I scattered them around the base of the waterfall. And I duly reported his death to the scientific community. I ordered extra equipment, installed it here myself when no one was looking. I rewired the building to the electrical grid. I came out to see my father, to bring him food, to assist in his work, but only late at night—after Mark and Kevin had gone to bed."

Suddenly—to Logan's shock—she reached out and clutched at his sleeve. "Do you see?" she asked in a tense tone. "Right or wrong, six months ago I had realized there was no way, *no way*, I would be able to save my father. He was as good as dead. . . . It was only a matter of time."

Laura's face looked drawn and utterly exhausted. She spoke more softly. "Jeremy, I'm not proud of this situation. But I hurt no one. That wanderer's death was tragic—but I took it as a sign. Only my father's 'death' would silence the taunting that tormented him so. And this way, he could continue his work in peace. And I can tell you, my father has been more productive—more like his old self—in this last half year than he's been in a decade. And I believe the world will benefit from his discoveries."

Suddenly, she looked at him once again with that same determination. "So . . . now what are you going to do?"

Logan didn't answer. He'd been so surprised to find Chase Feverbridge alive that this question had not yet occurred to him.

"We're at your mercy," she went on. "Both of us. But what you said the first time we met—about knowing what it's like to work, knowing the entire world might be laughing at you—makes me think you'll understand why I had to do what I did. You're an outsider—just as we are. You're not a cop. If you turn us in . . . well, I'm not going to try to stop you. But it's my hope you won't do that; that you won't judge us; that you'll understand. If you expose him to the world . . . it will be his death sentence. He'll try to commit suicide again—and this time, he'll succeed."

Logan opened his mouth to speak, then shut it again. He

realized he was facing a terrible quandary. Technically, Laura Feverbridge had done something illegal, or at the very least unethical—she had deliberately misidentified a body. On the other hand, it had been done with the best of intentions. The dead man had died accidentally, a lonely drifter with no family or social ties. The ashes had long since been scattered. He thought of the elderly Dr. Feverbridge, sitting inside the secret lab hidden deep in these woods. Even given the few words they'd exchanged, he'd felt an intellectual power, a charismatic conviction in his own beliefs, radiate from the man. He also sensed an alienness, a strangeness—exactly the kind of thing that would frighten men of smaller intellect: academics who'd be quick to dismiss his work. As Laura Feverbridge had reminded him, he himself was all too aware what it felt like to have one's work derided. He admired her loyalty—and he could sense the intense effort she had gone through, *was* going through, to help and protect her father. He'd been aware of something, that first time they'd met—something going on inside her that was beyond the ordinary. Now he knew what it was.

He also knew what Jessup would want him to do. But he asked himself: What crime had been committed here, really? And who had been hurt? Nobody. On the other hand, if he were to reveal the truth, the old man would quite likely take his own life . . . leaving his daughter alone and his work incomplete.

Laura Feverbridge was looking at him intently. He glanced from her face to the shotgun in her hands, and back into her eyes again. This was a dilemma he simply did not know how to resolve.

"Let's go back inside," he said.

She looked at him for a moment. Then she nodded and silently led the way across the clearing and into the lab.

20

As they stepped inside, Dr. Feverbridge—who was still sitting at the lab table—raised his head, looking at Logan with a mild yet proud gaze.

"I suppose my daughter told you all about me," he said. "The troubled genius, the self-destructive scientist."

Logan nodded silently as Laura Feverbridge placed the shotgun in a corner.

"I'm not proud that I tried to take my own life, Dr. Logan. But I simply couldn't stand it any longer—the personal anger, the despair." He paused. "I suppose I should consider myself the luckiest father in the world: to have a daughter willing to sacrifice so much for my sake. These past six months, I've been like a free man. You see, it doesn't matter to me whether my work is published posthumously, so to speak—it only matters that I get the chance to *finish* it, free from the constant, the *maddening,* torrent of hecklers and naysayers. Except it seems we've been careless of late. I suppose we've allowed our voices to be overheard, our lights to be seen."

"No doubt." Laura shook her head bitterly, then glanced at Logan. "And I suppose we have Kevin to thank for your return."

They had been keeping their voices pitched low, precisely so that—Logan realized—this same Kevin would not overhear them.

"The fact is, my work is extremely important. And I'm close to finishing it—so close." Feverbridge looked at Logan more intently. "I can sense you're conflicted. You don't know whether to alert the authorities about all this. Perhaps if I showed you the full nature of my work, showed you what we've truly accomplished, it would help you decide."

Laura looked at him sharply. "Father? Are you sure—?"

"What choice do we have? Besides, your Dr. Logan here might find our accomplishments enlightening." He looked back at Logan. "Let me pose a question to you. What do you suppose our early ancestors—the East African hominids—felt when they looked up at a full moon?"

Logan thought for a moment. "Fear."

"Precisely. To the average humanoid biped of two hundred thousand years ago, the full moon meant open season—and they were the game. For a predator like a saber-toothed tiger, the full moon would be like a spotlight shining on their prey. When people think of the 'lunar effect,' if they think of it at all, it's as a bunch of malarkey, an urban legend easily laughed away: surgeries going wrong, birthrates increasing, spikes in violent behavior, schizophrenics running amok. *National Enquirer* stuff." Feverbridge scoffed. "But the more I thought about it and studied it, the more I realized that the moon, especially the full moon, has in fact always exerted a truly *unexplainable* influence on earthly life, especially for diurnal animals. At first it presented as fear, as you just said yourself. Later, it was thought to cause madness, even lycanthropy." Here he gave a dismissive wave of a hand. "More recently, that has fallen aside—and today's science, as it does so often when it comes face-to-face with old beliefs and behaviors not easily understood by modern man, has turned its back. But the influence was there, nonetheless. And I became determined to understand what caused it."

He stood up and began to pace the room. "I read every paper, examined every account of the moon's influence. I attacked the problem from every angle: psychological, physiological, evolutionary. And though I could demonstrate that the full moon had, historically, an unusual influence, I could not discover the reason. Until I stumbled upon the Apollo moon landings."

This was so unexpected that Logan frowned. "I'm sorry?"

Feverbridge chuckled at Logan's discomfiture. "That's right. You know, of course, that when Apollo Eleven returned from the moon, it brought back many pounds of moon rocks, carefully packed in a metal box and sealed in such a way as to maintain the moon's low-pressure conditions. But when the astronauts landed back on earth, the seals on the box were gone. Ruined." He returned to the lab table, leaned in close to Logan. "And that's not all. Six times, Apollo missions returned with moon rocks in sealed containers. And six times, no matter what they tried, those seals on the containers were destroyed by the time they got back to earth." He paused. "Care to speculate why?"

Logan shook his head. "I can't even begin to speculate."

Feverbridge laughed again. "Dust."

"Excuse me?"

"Dust! Moon dust. You see, there's no wind on the moon. There's no water, there's no erosion—it's not like earth, where rocks and pebbles become smooth and rounded through abrasion. On the moon, dust is fine, but incredibly sharp, like a knife. It's essentially tiny, powdered glass. And it doesn't just cover the surface—it also floats like clouds, fifty miles or more above the surface, in the moon's exosphere. It rises up in streams—nobody knows exactly why, but some speculate that it's the 'fountain model': radiation from the sun knocking electrons from the atoms in the lunar dust, giving it a positive charge and causing it to rise on the solar wind. In 2013, NASA even sent a satellite—the Lunar Atmosphere and Dust Environment Explorer, or LADEE—to study this 'dust atmosphere.' It was intentionally crashed into the dark side of the moon six months later. As far as I know, the data is still being analyzed."

He pushed himself away from the table, began pacing again. "Ask yourself: what is moonlight? It's merely the sun's visible radiation, reflecting off the moon—*but being filtered through this strange cloud of moon dust.* When I analyzed it further, I discovered that, under the proper conditions, this dust changes the *quality* of the light: in distribution of wavelength and polarization—circular polarization, in fact. Those conditions include such violent activity as solar flares and the like. But I began to speculate further: Was it possible this unusual quality of light, when viewed by diurnal creatures on earth, could affect the brain sufficiently to cause changes in behavior? And could the full moon alone be enough to achieve that?"

Feverbridge walked to a large table set against the far wall, then motioned Logan toward him. "That was the beginnings of a working hypothesis: that the effect of this special, polarized moonlight, entering the brain, could cause an unusual response: fear, excitability, aggression. But, like any good scientist, I had to test this hypothesis. And that meant re-creating, not only moonlight, but moonlight filtered through the equivalent of moon dust, all within a laboratory environment. And that proved to be a very difficult and time-consuming process—at the time, hampered by my own mood of bitterness and defeat."

He paused a moment, looking carefully at Logan to see what impression his words were having. "But then, in secret, I moved to this lab. And work began in earnest, with new hope and enthusiasm. I started with moonlight itself. As you may know, all visible light has what's known as a color temperature, expressed in kelvins. Color temperatures over five thousand kelvins are known as 'cool' colors. The sun, which is similar to a standard blackbody radiator, emits light that penetrates our atmosphere at close to six thousand kelvins. The moon, a 'warmer' color, has a light temperature of around four thousand. The flame of a candle, for comparison, is closer to eighteen hundred kelvins."

He wheeled over the tall metal dolly holding the barrel-shaped lamp Logan had noticed when he'd first entered the building. "This luminaire is what's technically known as an HMI Fresnel light. The unique texturing of the Fresnel lens allows for an even light that 'softens,' or darkens, at the edges: much like our own perception of moonlight. HMI, or hydrargyrum medium-arc iodide—how's that for a mouthful!—produces light by means of an arc lamp instead of an incandescent bulb. They are extremely high-quality light sources—and extremely expensive. This one is particularly nice." He patted the light, which was half the size of an oil drum. It swung gently on its mount. "Goes for a cool twenty thousand dollars. It has an eighteen-K bulb that can throw a twelve-foot spot of fifteen hundred foot-candles almost seventy feet. Of course, I haven't used it at full strength—not for my current studies, at least. But suffice it to say rigorous analysis made it clear that this particular luminaire, at the proper setting, most closely approximates the way moonlight strikes the earth."

He walked over to a nearby shelf, pulled out a large plastic container, and placed it on the worktable. "Once I had achieved the proper temperature for moonlight, I had to simulate the effect of how the sun's photons would react when they pass through the moon's 'dust atmosphere,' bounce off the surface, and pass through the dust a second time on their way to the earth. This meant, first, researching the specific chemical nature of moon dust—which has been well documented by NASA—and then applying the precise filters to re-create it."

Swinging back the barn doors on the Fresnel, he opened the plastic container, removed a thin circular plate of pale glass, and fitted it to the front of the lens. He did this a second time, and then a third time, adding additional filters. Then he turned back to Logan. "This re-creates moonlight, as filtered through the dust atmosphere of the moon, as it would have been seen all over the earth five hundred years ago."

"Why five hundred years?" Logan asked.

"Because our atmosphere, Dr. Logan, has—over the last few centuries—become saturated with the burn-off of fossil fuels, greenhouse gases, what have you."

"In other words, the effect you hypothesize would have been much stronger in the past than it is today."

"Exactly: hence the many more eyewitness accounts of strange or unexplained behavior in early documents concerning the full moon. Now, please observe. I'm going to reproduce the effect of that same full moon." Walking over to the far wall, he picked up one of the animal cages, brought it over, and placed it on the table. "Northern short-tailed shrews," he explained. Then, reaching under the worktable, he pulled out a pair of heavy rubber gloves and put them on. "They're venomous," he went on, "but perfect mammals for our study." He opened the cage, reached inside, and pulled out first one, then another, of the guinea-pig-sized creatures, covered with soft gray fur. They sat on the table, sleepy and docile, evidently newly awakened.

"Now, watch carefully," Feverbridge said as he pulled the light stand back from the table and stood directly behind it.

"Don't look at the light," Laura Feverbridge warned, speaking for the first time since her father had begun his explanation. "Just the shrews."

She walked over to the wall and snapped off the overhead. Immediately, the room was plunged into darkness. A moment later, there was another snap, and the Fresnel came on, its spotlight aimed at the creatures on the worktable. The light, Logan noticed, was low, and of a pale, almost ghostly yellow—exactly like moonlight.

At first, nothing happened. Then the creatures began to show signs of restlessness. Within moments, this had turned to irritability. They began squabbling, emitting low squeaks and circling each other warily. Abruptly, one lunged at the other, which batted back with both sets of foreclaws.

Very quickly, Dr. Feverbridge turned off the Fresnel. At the same time, Laura snapped the overhead light back on. Immediately, the creatures returned to their docile state.

"Well?" Feverbridge said as he returned the creatures to their cage, then replaced it on the shelf.

"I—" Logan did not quite know what to say. It was all so unusual, so different from what he'd expected. Dr. Feverbridge and his daughter, he realized, were right: this was groundbreaking research—perhaps even revolutionary.

"You can reproduce this behavior at will?" he asked.

"On almost all occasions, yes. So far, we've only employed a variety of small mammals for our tests. I could repeat the procedure on a different species, if you wish—white mice, hooded rats, voles—but the result would be the same: marked deviation from normal behavior patterns."

"Why does this particular light affect the brain so strongly?" Logan asked.

"Remember the question I asked about early hominids? My belief is that it is an evolutionary development that's taken place over hundreds of thousands, perhaps millions, of years. Diurnal animals sleep at night to hide from predators, and the danger would be highest on the night of the full moon. It's become hard-wired into us. Subconsciously, the special quality of this light raises hormonal levels to a fever pitch. Adrenaline is dumped into the bloodstream; flight-or-fight behavior is triggered. Some creatures may flee. Others—like these shrews—become uncharacteristically aggressive . . . very aggressive. My own analysis shows that over the millennia, as our natural predators have died off, the aggressive behavior has become the norm."

"And if our atmosphere was to clear of smog and particulate matter? Would these deviant behaviors return when the moon is full—return to human beings, I mean?"

"Yes. Yes, I believe they would—depending, I suppose, on the person's physical and emotional makeup."

Logan tried to organize his thoughts; tried to process what he had just observed. "Kevin Pace, and the late Mr. Artowsky," he said. "Do they know about this?"

"Only indirectly. They are acting—were acting, in the case of poor Mark—as controls, studying the same creatures we are studying, but under normal atmospheric and environmental conditions."

Feverbridge turned away for a moment. When he turned back, the lighthearted, didactic mood was gone and anguish was suddenly in his eyes. "Do you understand the problem now, Dr. Logan? My theories have already been ridiculed to a degree that

I can no longer live with. What would they say if I released additional findings? I can see the taunting headlines now: 'Scientist claims space dust causes madness.' I couldn't bear that." The anguish on his face spiked. "I wouldn't."

"That's why we need to be as thorough as possible in completing the research," Laura Feverbridge said. She spoke in a calm, soothing voice. "Document everything. Continue as we have been, carefully, comprehensively. Amass sufficient evidence to pass any peer review they could throw at us. We're close now, Father. All we need is time. That is . . . if Dr. Logan will give it to us."

And with this, she fell silent. Both of them—father and daughter—looked at Logan.

Logan took a deep breath. This was clearly cutting-edge research. If it was halted prematurely, the world would be the poorer for it. And the world would also surely lose a brilliant scientist.

"Just give us a little time," Laura said, almost pleadingly. Coming forward, she gripped his sleeve again. "Time to finish our work. Then you can do whatever your conscience tells you."

Logan glanced from one to the other. He now realized something that had not occurred to him before: it was quite possible that the nature of this work could shed some light on the murders Jessup was trying so desperately to solve.

"I won't speak of this to anyone," he said in a low voice. "At least, not until the work is complete. It may help identify what's been going on out there in the woods. Meanwhile, if there's a way I can help you, I will."

For a long moment, the building was silent. Then Chase Feverbridge smiled faintly, nodded. Laura released her hold on his sleeve and took his hand in both of hers.

"Thank you," she said. "Thank you—for both of us."

21

In the days that followed, what he'd seen—and learned—at the secret laboratory in the woods behind the fire station left Logan in a state of moral uncertainty. There was no doubt that the elder Dr. Feverbridge's work was important. On the other hand, the manner in which he'd become, essentially, a walking dead man—although Logan fully understood the reasons for it—felt unsavory at best. However, the bottom line was that he simply could not, for the present, tell Jessup or anyone else about the circumstances. Not only would that put an end to the man's research—it would, almost certainly, put an end to his life.

As the days went on, and he once again grew fully involved in his own work, he became increasingly comfortable with simply staying on the sidelines and letting the police do their job. True to his promise, Jessup backed off; when Logan was again invited to the ranger's house for dinner, the conversation had focused solely on philosophy, French cuisine, and innocuous local gossip. Logan liked Suzanne already, and by dinner's end the two were almost like old friends. As far as Logan could tell, Jessup was toeing Krenshaw's line.

By the end of more than two additional weeks of solid effort, Logan managed to get most of the remaining work done on his monograph. His homebody behavior at Cloudwater clearly pleased Greg Hartshorn, the resident director, who—Logan now felt certain—had gotten wind of his inquiries into the recent deaths, to his evident displeasure.

One day, after driving into Saranac Lake for a few items, he ran into Harrison Albright, who had come into town to stock up at the local hunting and fishing store. Logan had enjoyed Albright's lecture and reading at Cloudwater and was relieved the man hadn't "ratted him out," and now offered to buy him lunch. Albright declined, saying that he subsisted almost entirely on rabbit and venison he bow-shot—and brandished a freshly purchased packet of arrows to prove it. He agreed to have coffee, however, and the two quickly fell into a lively discussion of poetry and literature. Logan found himself enjoying Albright's company: he had a truly unusual blend of literary education and a colorful life, combined with the outlook and skill of a born backwoodsman. Logan had never encountered anyone quite like him before. He stayed away from any questions about mysterious or unsettling forest lore, and Albright seemed to appreciate this in his rough-hewn way.

The only other times he ventured off the Cloudwater estate were, ironically, to visit the fire station where Laura Feverbridge had her lab. Despite his reservations about the old scientist's secret life, he felt himself drawn for reasons he did not quite understand to both father and daughter; Laura had a quick, eager scientific mind and, despite himself, he was impressed by how she had sacrificed for the sake of her father's well-being. The first visit was late one morning, when he found Laura alone in the main lab. They took a walk in the woods, chatting idly about how her work was proceeding, and—ironically—ended up at the base of Madder's Gorge, the spot where she'd found the body of the dead hiker. On the way back, she told Logan she presumed he'd like to speak with her father again, and suggested he come back late the following Friday, when Pace, the lab assistant, would be taking the weekend off. Logan agreed; he could not help but feel a growing admiration for this smart, compassionate, loyal, and dedicated woman.

On his next visit that Friday, Laura escorted him back to the secret lab, where Dr. Feverbridge was, it seemed, awaiting his arrival. Logan again asked about the work, and the older man eagerly described the progress he had made since they'd last met. Logan was struck once more by the man's brilliance and scholarly charisma. Freed at last from the carping of his would-be colleagues, he displayed none of the emotional frailty or despondency that Laura had described. In the course of discussing his work, he gave Logan an additional demonstration of how he could induce the lunar effect—this time on a nocturnal mammal, a fruit bat. Logan also learned there was a lab within the lab where he did some of his most cutting-edge work and that he insisted on keeping private, even from Laura. He explained how, once he'd finished the work to his satisfaction, he planned to let Laura publish it under her own name. "It's the least I can do, given all the sacrifices she's made for me," he said.

"And what will you do then?" Logan asked.

"I'll retire. This is my life's work, you understand, and it's almost done. I'll go someplace far away—I've always liked Ibiza. Or perhaps the Amalfi coast. Or maybe Santorini. A spot where I won't be surrounded by all of this," and he waved at the instrumentation with a smile. "Who knows? Maybe my reputation will be rehabilitated. Then again, maybe not. But by that point, I'll no longer care—*I'll* know, and Laura will know, that we've succeeded. That I've managed to make it to the end of the road. And that's the most important thing."

Logan thought of his own monograph, awaiting completion back at his cottage at Cloudwater, and nodded silently. He understood this sentiment completely.

22

The following evening, after Logan made his way back from the main lodge after dinner, he found Randall Jessup installed on the front porch of his cottage. The ranger was sitting on the front steps in the same spot where he'd found Pace, Laura Feverbridge's lab tech, waiting for him some two and a half weeks earlier.

"Randall," Logan said as the ranger stood to shake his hand. "Nice to see you. Come on in."

They stepped inside. Jessup took off his hat and hung it on the back of a chair, then took a seat on the wraparound sofa.

"Can I get you anything?" Logan asked. "Coffee, tea, something stronger?"

"Nothing, thanks."

Logan sat down opposite Jessup. He wondered what this visit could be about. He hadn't seen the ranger since the second dinner at the man's house, well over a week before. This certainly didn't feel like a social call. Quite the contrary: it was clear Jessup had something on his mind. There was a look on his face that could only be called troubled.

"Making any progress?" Logan asked, careful to give the question a light pitch.

"Not really. The search parties wrapped up without finding anything—no useful evidence, no rogue animal. We're basically waiting—and I don't like that at all."

"Waiting?"

"For the next full moon."

Logan nodded his understanding. *They haven't found the killer,* he thought. *So now they're waiting for it—or him—to strike again.* Logan knew such an approach would stick in Jessup's craw.

"When's it due?" he asked.

"The next full moon? Two days."

Two days. "But surely you've made some progress."

Jessup sighed. "Krenshaw still has a team of state troopers shadowing Saul Woden's cabin, just in case. And I've spent a fair amount of time in Pike Hollow, investigating the Blakeneys as best I can. Thin pickings, as you can imagine, although I do have what might be an unexpected lead. In any case, that's the spot— according to the locals, anyway, as you might guess—that trouble is most likely to come from. Krenshaw's keeping an eye on their compound, too."

"And what about you? Is that where you think the trouble's coming—if it comes at all?"

Instead of answering, Jessup asked a question of his own. "Tell me something, Jeremy. Why did you make a second visit to the scientific outpost at the fire station?"

The tickle of apprehension Logan felt at this unexpected question reminded him of his complicity. "How do you know about that?" he asked.

Jessup waved a hand, as if to say, *Let me have my few trade secrets.*

Logan thought quickly. "Second visit," Jessup had said. That meant he knew only of the two times Logan had been there during the day—not about his nocturnal visits. Unless he knew more than he was saying and was sifting his old friend for information. He looked closely at Jessup. But he didn't see any suspicion in the ranger's face. All he sensed was concern, frustration—and a degree of anxiety.

"The first time I went, it was to ask about Mark Artowsky, the lab assistant who was also the third victim. I met Laura Feverbridge. We talked a little about the nature of her work."

"Which is?"

"She's studying the lunar effect on small diurnal mammals."

"The lunar effect?" Jessup repeated.

"It's a theory that the moon, the full moon in particular, has an unusual influence on creatures. With people, for example, there are supposed spikes in the crime rate, more pregnancies, higher mortality during operations, things like that."

Although he felt a little guilty doing so, Logan deliberately mentioned the most sensational and unlikely phenomena associated with the lunar effect. He realized that he had a vested interest in minimizing the ranger's curiosity about the scientific outpost.

"Did she tell you what happened to her father?" Jessup asked.

"A little," Logan replied, not wanting to lie.

Jessup nodded. "That still doesn't explain your second visit."

"Why are you curious?"

"Indulge me."

Logan shrugged. "It's no secret. It was just a social call. It gets boring here, you know, writing and researching day after day. We took a short hike in the woods. I find her work interesting. I'm an enigmalogist, after all—something like the lunar effect is just my cup of tea."

"That's all that's going on there? Studying this lunar effect?"

"It's all I know about."

"Sounds like pseudoscience, if you ask me."

Logan allowed himself a small smile. "Well, I'm not only interested in her work. I'm interested in her."

Jessup had taken out his ever-present notebook, in preparation for jotting down a few items. Now he paused, raising his eyebrows. "I didn't take you for such a fast worker."

"Oh, I don't mean anything like that. We're just soul mates of a sort, working as we both do on the fringes of science."

Jessup nodded slowly. The troubled look had not left his face.

"What's bothering you, exactly?" Logan asked.

Instead of answering, Jessup slipped the notebook back into his pocket and stood up. Logan stood up as well. He felt torn between what he knew about Chase Feverbridge and what he was withholding from his friend. And yet he simply could not betray Laura—not only had he given his word, but he did not want to be held responsible for the old man's suicide.

"I don't know," Jessup said, intruding into Logan's thoughts. "Not for sure. Like I said, I might have an unexpected lead. Anyway, it's something I'm looking into. If I learn anything specific, perhaps I'll be more forthcoming." He walked to the door, then turned. "Just remember: we're only two days from another full moon. And there's something else to keep in mind—while a true full moon only lasts a moment, it appears to look full for at least three nights."

"Meaning?"

"Meaning only this: be very careful in the days to come, my friend." And with that, the ranger shook Logan's hand again, nodded, and stepped out the front door and into the night.

23

It was almost forty-eight hours later, to the minute, that Logan heard from Jessup again. His cell phone rang as he was sitting in the living room of his cabin, reading a draft of the closing argument of his monograph.

"Logan," he said as he answered the phone.

"Jeremy? It's Randall."

"Hi, Randall. What's up?"

There was a pause. "Jeremy, I don't know how to tell you this—how to *ask* you this."

The ranger's tone was oddly reserved, almost guarded. "Ask me what?"

"Do you remember our conversation of two nights ago? When

I told you that I was looking into something—and I'd say more if I learned anything specific?"

"Yes."

"Well, I have. And we should talk."

How odd. "Of course. Would tomorrow morning be good?"

"No—I think we should talk now. I'd like you to meet me."

Logan glanced at his watch: quarter to eight. "Tonight? What is it that can't wait?"

"I'll tell you when I see you."

"Very well. Where are you now—at home?"

"No. I'm on the far side of Pike Hollow, not far from the Blakeney place. You know Fred's Hideaway?"

"You mean that bar in Pike Hollow?"

"Yes. Can you meet me there as soon as possible?"

"If you really think it's that important, of course."

"Thanks. I'll be waiting for you in the Hideaway. I've got one or two things to check out, but I should still make it there before you."

Logan switched off his phone. For a moment he sat still, looking at it thoughtfully. Then, getting up, he shrugged into his jacket, reached for the keys to the Jeep. Then he stepped out of the cabin and began making his way down the path to the parking area.

Overhead, a full moon, bloated and yellow, hung in the crisp night sky.

24

It was a few minutes past eight when Sam Wiggins pulled onto 3A from the main street of Pike Hollow and headed west. His old Honda Civic—his barbershop business had not prospered of late, and he hadn't been able to buy a newer or larger vehicle after his thirty-year-old Ford pickup died the year before—jerked and rattled as it made its way down the rutted road. He looked up through the driver's window at the full moon, just visible through the screen of branches overhead, with a sinking feeling. On the seat beside him, Buster, his Jack Russell terrier, whined and whimpered.

This was crazy, he knew. All other residents of Pike Hollow, as if by unspoken consent, were locked in their houses, shutters closed, lights extinguished. And here he was, heading out toward

Desolation Mountain. Well, okay, not exactly *toward* Desolation Mountain, but a lot closer to it than he'd like to be.

It was all the fault of his aunt Gertrude, who lived in an old Airstream trailer out in the woods about eight miles west of Pike Hollow. She had no car, and she relied on Sam to bring her canned foodstuffs, cash her welfare checks, bring her pitiful mail from the PO box, fill her propane tank—and, most particularly, keep her well stocked with the cheap plastic 1.75-liter bottles of vodka that she subsisted on. Gertrude Randowsky was the most raging of all alcoholics Sam had ever known, and it had only gotten worse once her husband died and could no longer keep her in check. She'd run out of the stuff again, and it was only the threat of her towering rage that had coaxed Sam to get Fred at the Hideaway to give him half a dozen bottles and head out to the trailer.

Buster was whining more loudly now. Well, Sam could hardly blame him.

He passed the old Blakeney compound—a narrow lane to the left, heavily overgrown, dark and unoccupied state trooper car barely visible in the moonlight—with trepidation. That bitch Gertrude. She wasn't even his own aunt, she was the aunt of his late wife . . . and yet here he was, bowing and scraping to her every whim like a damn lackey. One of these days, he thought grimly as he rounded first one bend, and then another, those bottles of Olde Petersburg Vodka would do her in—and, although he'd never say it out loud, that day couldn't come soon enough, and he could then devote all his off-hours to making caddis fly lures and fishing for the elusive brook trout. . . .

Wham. *Shit, what was that—a blowout?* Oh God, this was the last place he wanted to have to change a tire.

He slowed the Honda, then crept forward gingerly. The right front end was shimmying like crazy, all right. He stopped and turned off the engine, leaving the headlights on, thinking. He had three options: get out and swap the tire for a spare; try driving home on the rim; or just abandon the car and walk back.

He immediately discarded the last option. No way was he walking back to Pike Hollow past the Blakeneys—not during a full moon, and with the state trooper who was supposed to be surveilling it off having dinner or something. And driving on a rim seemed almost as bad an option, incurring expenses he could ill afford to pay. With a sigh, he reached for the glove compartment, opened it, pulled out the flashlight he kept inside, and—reluctantly—opened the driver's door.

Swallowing painfully, he stood by the door, looking around, senses on full alert, ready to jump back in and lock the door if anything seemed amiss. There was a break in the trees overhead and the moon was in view, almost comically large, the pellucid night sky allowing a veil of pale yellow to fall over his surroundings. There was no wind, and the numberless trees that surrounded him were standing, almost as if at attention, awaiting something.

Leaving the driver's door open, he switched on the light and walked around the hood, glanced left and right again, then knelt to inspect the tire. To his relief, it seemed to be all right after all—it was just stuck in a huge rut that ran along the shoulder of the cracked highway. He must have drifted into it without noticing.

He stood up. Time to get this damn-fool errand over with and hurry home.

But just as he began to make his way back around the hood, something short and hairy shot between his legs, whimpering, heading into the darkness away from the car. *Buster.* He'd jumped out of the front seat while Sam had been inspecting the tire and run off.

"Well, if that don't beat all . . ." Buster wasn't Rin Tin Tin, but he had plenty of pluck, and it wasn't like him to run away—and it sure as hell wasn't like him to desert his master. Something must have scared him—scared him enough to make him forget all his normal instincts.

It had not gone unnoticed by Sam that Buster had run into the woods in the opposite direction from the Blakeney compound.

"Buster!" he called, beginning to walk in the direction the dog had run, toward the dark wall of trees. *"Bus—"*

Suddenly he stopped in mid-call. Some instinct told him to be silent—silent as the grave.

He turned off his flashlight. Now there were only the headlights of the car and the glow from the open door.

At first he noticed nothing unusual. But then he became aware of a strange smell—more of a stink, really: musky, rank.

This was followed by a noise unlike anything Sam had ever heard before: something between the menacing snarl of a feral wolf and the guttural, angry grunt of a bull moose. And it sounded close.

Sam Wiggins had lived in Pike Hollow his entire life. He'd grown up on stories of strange things in the deep woods like other children grew up on Mother Goose and Peter Rabbit. Over the years, he'd come to accept them as gospel—in some form or another—and taken steps to avoid them. And so he had managed never before to come face-to-face with the actual sound, or smell, of evil. There was a long moment when he stood, paralyzed with surprise and fear. He felt a warm gush as his bladder let go.

The stench grew stronger: fetid, sour, goatish. There was a crackling in the brush near the side of the road. And then he heard that sound again. It was husky and ravenous: ravenous for blood and the rending of flesh.

Suddenly, a hundred things seemed to happen at once. Sam

abruptly found his feet again and dashed around the front of the car, literally diving inside as a loud crashing burst from the nearby bracken; at the last possible moment he reached back and pulled the door closed, punching the lock as he did so; his flashlight, falling to the floor of the passenger seat, rolled backward and he saw something outside the window that, temporarily, drove all rational thought from his mind. Neighing in terror and dismay, he cringed back, windmilling with his legs, while the thing outside beat on his car with unimaginable fury. And then the light seemed to grow in intensity; the roaring sound suddenly mingled with another; his car shook once again under the violent assault— and then Sam slumped over the center column of the Civic, fainting, as merciful oblivion overtook him.

25

It took Logan longer than expected to reach Pike Hollow. Unlike on his earlier sorties, this time there was some traffic on the road—a ramshackle old truck with wood-framed sides, apparently hauling a variety of mechanical trash—and it seemed incapable of going faster than thirty miles an hour. Logan was unable to pass on the dark, twisty roads. To his relief, it continued down the main highway at the junction with 3A, and—turning onto the secondary road—he was able to make up some time. Even so it was almost nine as he neared the hamlet.

But just as he approached the turnoff for Pike Hollow, he noticed—ahead, around the bend in the road—a riot of flashing red and blue lights. Curious, he continued past the turnoff and drove around a few curves in the road.

A remarkable sight confronted him. On the shoulder some two hundred yards ahead of the third bend were no less than three state police cars and two ambulances, all with their lights whipping frantically. Dark figures could be seen moving beyond the vehicles, and powerful torches flashed over the blackness of the forest wall.

Feeling a sudden, deep misgiving, Logan immediately pulled off the road and killed both his engine and headlights. He sat there for a moment, observing the scene. He could hear a fugue of muttered conversations, with one particularly strident, anguished voice erupting occasionally over the drone before relapsing into silence. As he watched, Logan saw the oversized form of Krenshaw lumber in front of one pair of headlights before disappearing into the darkness again.

Even from this distance, he felt a terrible foreboding wash over him. Nevertheless he eased his way out of the Jeep, closed the door, and began approaching—stealthily, keeping to the shoulder, staying out of sight of the troopers, especially Krenshaw. As he drew closer, he could see two additional vehicles. One was an official park ranger truck. It looked like Jessup's. The driver's door was open. Directly in front of it was a beat-up old foreign sedan. "Beat-up" was an understatement: even from his vantage point, Logan could see the car was a wreck: huge dents in the roof, hood, and side panels; star-shaped impact marks in the windshield. A man was sitting on the far side of the hood, clothes askew, slumped forward, surrounded by several state troopers with notebooks and recorders in hand.

The sense of foreboding grew stronger.

He was now close to the emergency vehicles, and he could see a knot of EMTs bending over what looked like a shredded jumble of clothing and raw meat. Another step forward—and suddenly, as an official moved out of a spotlight, the scene resolved itself with terrifying clarity. He saw the unmistakable ranger's hat, some distance away, its usual olive green now dark and matted with gore. What had seemed like a disordered heap of bloody clothing was, in fact, a body—a body torn almost beyond resemblance to humanity. Logan made out a ranger's shoulder patch among the shredded remains. And then—to his dismay and horror—he saw, at one end of the jumble, the head of his friend Randall Jessup. It was dreadfully lacerated and misshapen . . . but it was nevertheless unmistakable. The eyes were open, and in the scene-of-crime lights they seemed to be staring directly at him.

"Hey!" Logan was shocked out of his paralysis by a shout. He looked over to see Krenshaw, who had spotted him and was quickly coming over. "This is a crime scene," he snapped. Despite an awful daze that threatened to overwhelm him, Logan could see that Krenshaw looked more than usually angry. More than that: the man seemed uncharacteristically anxious.

"Get back," he said roughly as he stepped up to Logan, preparing to bodily push him away. But Logan just stood there, head now turned away from the grisly sight yet somehow unable to move.

He heard Krenshaw sigh, then mutter a curse. The trooper let his arms drop to his sides. "Yes," he said after a moment. "It's Jessup."

"What happened?" Logan heard himself ask.

Krenshaw paused before replying. "All right. This one time, I'll tell you what we know—because you were a friend of his, went to school together. Otherwise you'd get fuck-all from me. It seems he was heading east, to Pike Hollow. He stopped here when he saw an assault in progress on the occupant of that Civic."

"What kind of an assault?" Logan asked woodenly.

"That's what we're trying to find out. The victim isn't being too helpful, as you can hear for yourself." As if on cue, the man sitting on the edge of the hood began to gesticulate wildly, his hands waving about as if to ward off something terrible. He uttered a brief, shrieking scream.

Despite his grief, horror, and growing feeling of numbness, Logan forced himself to ask another question—knowing it would probably be his only chance to do so. "Saul Woden?"

"According to my men, the guy never left his house this evening. On the other hand, there was plenty of noise coming out of the Blakeney compound."

"What kind of noise?"

"I don't know. My first man here on the scene couldn't describe it all that well. Strange shit. A howling, he said—but not like any howling he'd heard before. Crashing sounds." Krenshaw, who himself had developed something of a thousand-yard stare, now drew himself up. "And now you'll have to leave, Dr. Logan. Don't force me to have you escorted from the scene."

After a moment, Logan nodded. Krenshaw began to walk away. A trooper came up to him and Krenshaw immediately began demanding the badge number of the trooper who'd left his vehicle outside the Blakeney residence so he could go into Pike Hollow for a bite of dinner. Next, they began discussing whether there was a back entrance to the Blakeney compound and, if so, how they could access it. Just as he was turning away, Logan heard the man sitting on the hood of the Civic raise his voice again. Looking back, he saw that the man had risen to his feet and was being restrained by two state troopers. With fresh surprise, he recognized the man as Sam the barber, who had given him a haircut on his first visit to Pike Hollow.

"I don't know what it was!" he was saying, his voice growing louder and ragged. "Stop asking me! Why do you keep asking me? It was like a man, but larger, hairy, and it ran along the ground like a dog, or a wolf maybe. It had red eyes and a terrible . . . no, you can't make me say it! It was wrecking the car, trying to beat in the window to get at me . . . and then the ranger pulled up and got out of his truck, but it moved so fast it was on top of him before he could pull out his gun, and then it wouldn't stop, it wouldn't stop, and . . . God, my God, *no, NO . . . !*"

And as Logan made his way back to the Jeep on stiff legs that weren't his own, the screaming started up again—and this time it did not stop.

26

That night, Logan slept very little, shock and grief forcing him to toss restlessly. Again and again he replayed in his mind the horrible images he'd witnessed on the shoulder of the highway. It seemed almost impossible to believe. Randall Jessup, gone—killed by the very thing he had been hunting; the very thing, apparently, he had approached Logan about on his first night at Cloudwater.

Finally, feeling the need to divert his mind with something else, he got up and, sitting down at his laptop, managed to put the final touches on his monograph on medieval heresy.

It was exactly eight o'clock in the morning when he completed the last sentence.

Even given the dismal circumstances, it seemed that some sort of ceremonial event, no matter how small, was necessary to mark the occasion. And so, while Cloudwater always laid on a lavish breakfast, he decided to drive into Ray Brook and the one pastry shop in the area he'd found that served passable croissants. After that, he would stop by the Jessup house to pay his respects to Suzanne. It was true he didn't know her well—he had met her only twice—but he was clearly Jessup's oldest friend in the region, and it seemed the right thing to do.

Ninety minutes later, leaving the pastry shop and heading for Saranac Lake, he passed the low building that housed Region 5 of the New York State Forest Rangers HQ—the place he'd heard Krenshaw's briefing on the details of Artowsky's death. It looked far different from the first time he'd seen it: now it appeared to be mobilizing for D-Day. Several Hummers, ATVs, and what looked like some kind of semi-military vehicle in camouflage were parked outside, and both rangers and state police were moving back and forth with antlike industry. Among them, Logan spotted the tall, powerfully built man Jessup had introduced to him as Jack Cornhill, the supervisor of Zone C. Logan guided his jeep into the parking lot and stopped beside the man.

Cornhill stared at him for a moment before recognition dawned. When it did, the guarded expression on his face morphed to a weary sadness. "You're Randall's friend, right?" he asked.

Logan nodded.

"Terrible thing." Cornhill shook his head. "That's an awful way for anybody to go, but a man like Randall . . ." His voice died away for a moment. "Nice wife, too. Really smart. And those sweet kids . . ." He shook his head again.

Logan indicated the cluster of vehicles and the activity that surrounded them. "What's with all the muscle?"

"Well, with this fourth murder—that of a law officer, too—Krenshaw is through with half measures."

"In other words, he's going to raid the Blakeney compound."

Cornhill hesitated a moment, then nodded. "That's right. He's going to raid it—and hard."

"When?"

Cornhill shrugged. "Day after tomorrow, maybe. Next day at the latest. Depends on how long it takes Krenshaw to get organized." He pointed at the vehicles. "As you can see, he doesn't waste time. He's calling in troops from as far away as Glens Falls."

Logan thanked the ranger, said good-bye, and continued on his way to the Jessup residence.

He paused outside the driveway of the neat, small, freshly painted house. It looked just the same as before: he could almost imagine Jessup, mentally communing with Emerson and the other transcendentalists as he nailed the clapboards and laid the shingles with his own hands. It seemed hard to imagine that the man who had built this house, who had fathered the family that lived within, was gone. But gone he was—death had visited this tidy home with a vengeance.

Two vehicles he did not recognize were in the driveway. One was an official New York State Forest Ranger truck that was just pulling out as he arrived. The other was a light-colored sedan. He waited in the Jeep for about fifteen minutes, not wishing to disturb whoever was inside with Suzanne, mentally composing what comforting words he could offer. And then the front door opened and a middle-aged woman emerged. She embraced a figure within—it was too dark to make out any features—and then walked to the sedan, dabbing at her eyes with a tissue as she did so.

Logan waited for the woman to drive away. He waited another five minutes to let Jessup's family have a little time for themselves.

He realized he was stalling: this was the last thing he wanted to do. Heaving a sigh, he started the engine and drove up to the house.

Suzanne Jessup answered the door. No one else appeared to be home. Her honey-colored hair was askew; her eyes were puffy and red-rimmed. For a moment, she just looked at him blankly. And then her face crumpled. "Oh, *Jeremy*," she said, and threw her arms around him.

"I'm so sorry," he murmured as he led her inside. She let him steer her toward a sofa, let him sit her down, as if she had no will of her own. She began to weep: deep, violent, racking sobs that—as he continued to embrace her—shook them both.

"He was my best friend," she said. "My soul mate in everything. Everything. How could this happen?"

Logan decided the best response was simply to hold her; to let her speak. He certainly was not about to tell her he'd seen how Jessup had died.

"The kids are away," she sobbed. "Vacationing with my parents in Pound Ridge. How am I going to tell them their father is dead?"

"It's unfair," he replied. "Horribly unfair. Nobody should have to do such a thing—ever. When are they due back?"

She released her hold on him, sat back. "Tomorrow. My father is driving them up."

"Then I think you need to tell them tonight. They need to start to grieve, and the journey home might be the best time for that to begin. You don't want them to arrive expecting to see him."

She pulled a tissue from a box on a nearby table. "You're right. But Jeremy, they adored him so. . . ." And with this she started weeping again.

"And they always will. That will never change. Randall was a wonderful friend to me. I know he was a wonderful father and husband. That's a legacy your kids—and you as well—can always cherish. Children are stronger than we give them credit for, you know. . . . In some ways, they're stronger than we are."

Suzanne sniffed, nodded.

The doorbell rang. "That must be Betty Cornhill," Suzanne said, dabbing at her eyes with a tissue. "She said she'd stop by around now."

This, Logan assumed, was Jack Cornhill's wife. "I'll be on my way," he said. "I just wanted to stop by and let you know how sorry—"

"No," Suzanne interrupted. "No—stay, please. I want to hear your stories about Randall: how you met, how you became friends, what he was like at college. I need to hear more, learn something about him I didn't know before—does that make any sense?"

Logan nodded. It made perfect sense.

"His office is right down the hall." Suzanne stood up, still dabbing at her eyes and leading the way. "You can wait in there."

"Very well." Logan let himself be ushered into a small, neat office-cum-den. He heard Suzanne's retreating steps; heard the front door open; heard a susurrus of female voices, followed by renewed weeping.

27

Logan looked around the room. Its contents brought the memory of his old friend back to him with a fresh pang of grief. The shelves, on which books about forestry and wildlife management sat cheek by jowl with philosophical treatises. The tidy desk, with its computer and small neat piles of papers. The bust of Thoreau that Jessup had kept near at hand ever since his senior year in college. Several framed photographs, carefully arranged on the walls: a young Jessup, wearing a backpack, tanned and smiling, in some exotic eastern location. A much more mature Jessup, straddling the roof beam of this very house, one victorious hand holding up a hammer, apparently just having finished construction. Jessup the family man, posing with Suzanne and the kids in front of what looked like Mirror Lake, the buildings of Lake Placid rising up behind.

His eyes wandered absently across the top of the desk. They stopped when they reached Jessup's battered leather-bound notebook, lying beside the computer. This was surprising: Logan had never known Jessup to go anywhere without that notebook peeping out of his breast pocket.

Only one voice could be heard now in the living room: low and consoling. Logan stared at the notebook. What had Jessup's last words been to him, over the phone, when he'd asked for the meeting in the Pike Hollow bar? *Jeremy, I don't know how to tell you this—how to ask you this. Do you remember our conversation of two nights ago? When I told you that I was looking into something—and I'd say more if I learned anything specific? Well, I have. And we should talk.*

He reached out, let his fingertips brush the cover of the journal. Then he picked it up. He felt a tinge of voyeurism—but also intense curiosity. Suzanne wanted to hear stories about her dead husband's past; Logan wanted to know what had been occupying the ranger's thoughts in the present.

He began paging through the journal. It was not the typical law officer's log: jotted facts and dry observations were interspersed with quotes from Jessup's favorite thinkers—on an early page, Logan came across G. K. Chesterton's observation, "The one created thing which we cannot look at is the one thing in the light of which we look at everything." As Logan continued to leaf through the notebook, the entries became increasingly focused on the recent killings: the condition of the bodies, where they were found, summaries of official briefings. There was also, he noticed, an entry describing Logan's own aborted attempt to visit the Blakeney compound, and what he'd reported about his initial visit to Pike Hollow. But then, on the last page, the carefully penned, methodically entered notes gave way to a series of fragments and questions:

C. Feverbridge—died April 16. Direction of final research

Jeremy and Laura Feverbridge—? Not hearing whole story!

Lunar effect??

Albright: F. & Blakeneys

He closed the journal and put it down. What these fragments meant, exactly, Logan did not know—but it appeared that Jessup had been focusing on him, and on the Feverbridges, almost as much as on the degenerate Blakeneys. He wasn't sure, but it seemed that his explanations of why he'd been visiting the old fire station had not completely satisfied his old friend.

Jeremy, I don't know how to tell you this—how to ask you this. I think we should talk now.

Jessup had discovered something. That was why he did not bring his notebook with him the night before. He wasn't planning to meet in order to interrogate Logan further, but to tell him something.

He let his eyes continue roaming over the desk as he tried to parse this sudden and surprising development. Now his eyes stopped on the screen of the computer. It showed two browser windows, each containing what appeared to be a scholarly paper. To his astonishment, Logan saw that the papers were written by Chase Feverbridge.

Eyes not moving from the screen, he sat down at the desk and began to read. Both articles, it seemed, had appeared in less-than-reputable publications: perhaps the best, or only, scientific organs in which Feverbridge could lately get his work disseminated.

He read through both from beginning to end. The first article, actually more of an extract than a full-blown paper, had been published late the previous year and discussed how Feverbridge planned to demonstrate, through conclusive proof, that elements in the moon's atmosphere were the direct cause of the "lunar effect." The second—and last, having been published this last February—dealt with transformational biology and regrowth: the macrophages that permitted a salamander to regrow a lost limb; the "imaginal discs" that allowed a caterpillar to transform into a butterfly, even once enzymes had dissolved many of its tissues. The article concluded with speculation about potential ways in which animal DNA could be used to influence, if not directly modify, human DNA and its genetic code—and how such changes could perhaps be precipitated in the laboratory.

Logan sat back in the chair. No wonder Laura Feverbridge had spoken of her father being the object of withering scorn. The first article reflected in vague terms Feverbridge's recent experiments with the quality and duplication of moonlight and its influence on behavior, which he'd seen firsthand, but the second—with its talk of bizarre transformational effects—was no doubt what had really made him an object of ridicule. Perhaps coming under severe academic fire had forced him to reconsider such radical speculation and—in the wake of his aborted suicide and apparent death, which in a sense gave him a new lease on life—Feverbridge had scaled back the nature of his experiments and concentrated on proving the argument made in his first paper.

One thing was clear: Jessup had been on a journey of discovery that Logan himself should, if he was honest with himself, already have made. With his eidetic memory, he recalled Laura Feverbridge's words: *And then, he published those last two articles . . . but he did it prematurely, submitted without my knowledge, promising much in the text but without the necessary scientific underpinnings and relevant data. I guess he was lashing out at his detractors, trying to prove his point. The result was precisely the opposite he'd hoped for—he was subjected to academic ridicule even more severe. It was then that he . . . tried to kill himself.*

The first thing he should have done, he now realized, was consult those articles she'd mentioned—if only for the sake of comprehensiveness. But then, at the time he'd been too shocked by the discovery that Dr. Feverbridge was still alive, and too impressed by the laboratory results he'd been shown, for her passing reference to her father's last articles to truly register.

He wondered just what Randall had discovered, and what he'd planned to tell him at the Hideaway. Was he planning to confront Logan about the Feverbridges? Was it possible he'd learned the father was still alive? No—that didn't seem likely. What could he have wanted to tell Logan so badly it could not wait for the following day? He sighed: now it did not seem like he would ever know.

But wait: there had been another fragmentary entry in the last page of Jessup's notebook—one that Logan understood even less. *Albright: F. & Blakeneys . . .*

The voices from the living room increased in volume; there was the sound of an opening door. Quickly, Logan rose from the chair, pushed it back up to the desk. He considered closing the browser windows, but left them untouched out of respect for his dead friend. A moment later, Suzanne appeared in the doorway to the office. Her eyes were even redder now, but a small, sad smile was on her face.

Logan followed her back out to the living room with a mind deeply troubled.

28

When he left the Jessup residence, about half an hour later, the inner turmoil had not left him. Glancing at his image in the rearview mirror, he reflected that he was now finished—and yet, on the other hand, he was not finished. True, his monograph was complete. But Jessup, who had asked him in person to look into the peculiar circumstances regarding the recent murders, was still asking—only now the voice was quieter, and Logan could no longer see him. The request remained, however—and the ranger's own death had given it a new urgency that Logan could no longer ignore.

And so he did not turn in at the entrance to Cloudwater, but instead drove past the artists' colony and continued down State Highway 3, taking the turnoff to 3A and heading toward Pike

Hollow. A few miles short of the hamlet, he pulled in at the rustic A-frame set back from the road, red pickup in the driveway.

Albright answered the door on the second rap. It was almost as if he'd been expecting someone. And there was no surprise in his clear blue eyes at seeing Logan, either. Wordlessly, he motioned for Logan to take a seat in one of the hand-carved chairs, then sat down himself. He'd been whittling something out of a piece of pine with his massive hunting knife; looking closely, Logan saw that it was a long-gowned woman, apparently holding a lyre.

"Euterpe?" he asked, hazarding a guess.

Albright nodded. "Muse of lyric poetry." He shaved off a few more parings, then dropped the knife and the carving onto the floor beside his chair.

"Did you hear about Randall Jessup?" Logan asked.

Albright nodded. Despite the chill weather, he wore a chambray shirt with the sleeves rolled up, and as he scratched his thick white beard the muscles in his forearm knotted like whipcord. "I feel real bad about that."

Logan didn't know exactly how to begin. Albright, he was sure, was the connection he sought—but in what way exactly, or whether the tough, reserved mountain man would be forthcoming, he couldn't begin to guess.

"He called me up, last night," Logan said. "He'd been looking into the recent murders, of course—and, as I told you, he'd been asking me to do the same. After some investigation I'd told him that I couldn't help. But he'd discovered something—that much was clear. He wanted to meet at the Hideaway, right away. He had something to tell me."

Albright said nothing; he merely listened, still slowly scratching his beard.

"I stopped by his house this morning, to do what I could to

comfort Suzanne. While I was there, I happened to find Randall's journal—the one he jotted all his case notes in. The last entries were very curious. My name was mentioned. So was that of Chase Feverbridge. The final entry is why I'm here. It read: 'Albright: F. & Blakeneys.' "

Albright stopped scratching and let his hand drop to his dungarees. "Randall was a good man. And a good ranger. That philosophical bent of his: it helped him see things in ways other rangers couldn't—helped him ask the hard questions, the unusual questions." He paused a moment, as if taking the measure of Logan with his eyes. "He stopped by to see me yesterday, too," he said. "He did that now and then: if he had a problem he wanted to bounce off an objective listener—hard to find in these parts—or just talk about poetry or the lure of the deep woods. But he hadn't come to chat this time. He came loaded with questions: about Laura Feverbridge. About you, too. And about the Blakeneys. And that's when I told him."

"Told him what?"

Albright picked up the knife again, began cleaning his fingernails with its edge. "Guess I'd better tell you, too—under the circumstances. Randall's dead; he can't tell you himself. See, I've been trying to stay out of this whole mess ever since the first body was found. It's like I told you the first time we met: I've heard some pretty outlandish backwoods tales, both growing up and since moving back here, and these murders . . . well, they were no 'tale.' And they felt wrong to me. That's the only word I can use for them. Not just cruel, vicious, bizarre—but wrong."

Wrong. Jessup had used the same word, that first night he described the killings in Logan's cabin. And it was the same word that had come to Logan's mind, more than once.

"Murders like these stir people up. Get them thinking things, suspecting things. I didn't want to add fuel to the fire. Besides, it wasn't any of my business. And from what I heard, the poor man had been subject to enough criticism and second-guessing during his lifetime. Why trouble his rest?"

Logan thought back to Jessup's final scrawled notes. "You're talking about Dr. Feverbridge."

"Did you know he wrote poetry, too? Not the kind I write—and not the kind I'd care to read, either. But you have to admire a scientist who does any versifying at all. Besides, I liked the way he fought against his critics, the way he raged against the world, even though the effort to do so broke his will."

"How do you know this?" Logan asked.

"We met a couple, three times. Sort of hit it off. Don't ask me why—two more different men were never born. He came to a reading I did in Lake Placid. Hung around afterward and we got to talking. Some time later, I stopped by the fire station where he had his lab. This was early in the spring, and I do a fair amount of hunting for wild hare around those parts after the first thaw. Must have been a month or so before his death. He talked about his work—can't say I understood it. And that's when I learned we had something in common."

"What was that?"

"The Blakeneys."

Logan sat forward in his chair. "*What?*"

"Oh, they're not quite as ornery and standoffish as they put on. There's one or two folks that they tolerate, more or less. It's true they don't like strangers, and there's no love lost between them and the good citizens of Pike Hollow—the bad blood goes back too far for that to ever change. And they have a good reason to keep to themselves."

"What's that?" Logan asked.

But Albright didn't answer directly. "Dr. Feverbridge told me he'd managed to make the acquaintance of the clan—exactly how, I don't know. Maybe the same way I initially did: on the off chance you run into one, treat him respectable, don't get all judgmental and curious. But if you want my real opinion, I think it had to do with money—that's something the Blakeneys could always use a lot more of, no matter how self-sufficient they might seem. No doubt he'd heard the rumors about them and grown curious. Anyway, he'd been a visitor at their compound—once, maybe twice; Feverbridge grew vague with the details when I started asking questions." He slipped the knife back into the scabbard. "And that's what I told Jessup, when he stopped by here yesterday afternoon. And *that's* when Jessup told me how curious he was about what Feverbridge had been working on: the lunar effect, I think they both called it."

Logan was silent. He couldn't tell Albright that Feverbridge was still alive; that would be breaking his promise to Laura and to the scientist himself. His mind worked fast, trying one theory after another but rejecting each in turn. That Feverbridge had visited the Blakeneys—that *anyone* had visited them—was a surprise: but why was it important? Then he recalled the articles he'd seen displayed on Jessup's desk—and it was as if a key had just slid into a lock.

Albright said nothing, but his expression implied an understanding that some revelation, or partial revelation, had taken place. "You've been out to the Feverbridge lab," he said.

"Yes."

"Seen those dogs of his?"

"The Weimaraners? Yes."

"Awful big, aren't they?"

Logan didn't reply, and after a moment Albright spoke again. "Anyways, now you know why I feel bad about Jessup's death."

"Why? You don't think your telling him that fact could possibly have anything to do with his death?"

Albright shrugged.

"His death has had one result, though. The leader of the task force, a trooper named Krenshaw, is planning to raid the Blakeney compound."

At this, Albright's bushy eyebrows shot up. "When?"

"Soon. Perhaps the day after tomorrow."

Albright stood up, dusted the wood curlings from his lap. "Then I guess we'd better go pay a call."

Logan glanced up at him. "Where?"

"The Blakeneys. Who else?" And as he spoke, the man shrugged into a faded hunting jacket.

29

Logan rose slowly to his feet. Albright glanced over at him, chuckling at his obvious discomfiture.

"We're going to pay a social visit on the people who stuck a shotgun in my face the last time I went calling," Logan said.

"Not a social visit, exactly," Albright replied. "But I think it's time you found out just what kind of people they really are. They need to know about this raid the troopers are planning—I owe them that much. Besides, isn't there something you want to ask them?"

"What's that?" Logan asked.

"Why Dr. Feverbridge visited their compound."

Logan glanced at him for a minute. Over the past twenty-four hours, the shocks and the tragic events had followed so closely, one upon the other, that he now felt tired and almost stupefied. But immediately, he realized the man was right. He'd come to see Albright because he'd believed, at some instinctual level, that the man was the connection he sought to what Jessup had uncovered: and he'd been right. That connection was Dr. Feverbridge, and why he had struck up an acquaintance with the Blakeney clan, of all people—the very group that all the locals hated, mistrusted, and suspected of murder.

"Of course," he said. "But will they talk to me?"

"Maybe. If I'm with you."

"Very well. But aren't you going to take that?" And Logan nodded toward a .20-06 rifle that hung over the rough stone fireplace.

"No, sir. That would just agitate them." And he led the way out the front door.

The passenger seat of Albright's pickup was loaded with an assortment of junk—waders, a few knives of various sizes, a crossbow and assorted quarrels, a torn and faded army jacket with a sergeant's patch on one shoulder, a box of fishing tackle. Albright threw it all into the backseat and Logan climbed in. Firing up the engine, Albright backed out of the driveway, then started west down 3A. Logan glanced at his watch: it was quarter past two.

They passed the turnoff for Pike Hollow and, after another bend in the road, the overgrown entrance to the Blakeney compound. Three state trooper vehicles were now blocking it.

"How are we going to get past that welcoming committee?" Logan asked.

"We're not going in the front door," Albright explained.

A few more bends in the road brought them to the site where Jessup had met his death. Crime scene tape was still strung around a large area of the shoulder. Logan stared at it as they passed by, horror and sorrow mingling within him.

Albright drove the truck around one more bend, and then— veering across the center stripe—pulled onto the oncoming shoulder and then into what to Logan appeared an impenetrable wall of brush. It was, however, only a foot or two deep—the truck pushed its way through and into a small clearing, barely large enough for the vehicle, surrounded on all sides by thick forest. The shrubbery sprang back into position behind them, effectively hiding the truck from the road. Albright shut off the engine, then jumped out, and Logan followed his example.

"Ready?" Albright said.

Logan nodded. Albright walked around the front of the truck and stepped into what was seemingly an unbroken line of trees and heavy vegetal undergrowth. As they began penetrating deeper, however, Logan realized they were following a path of sorts—unmarked, barely visible, but nevertheless of human construction. It was so faint and narrow that he could never have followed it himself. Branches of pine needles brushed across his face as he stayed close behind Albright.

"How can you navigate this without a compass?" he asked. Albright's only answer was a scoff.

The path twisted and turned with the varying topography of the forest floor, now rising to a height of land, now descending into a valley. Sunlight barely filtered through the heavy canopy overhead. Albright never stopped to check his position, but kept up a steady pace.

"I first met Nahum Blakeney in these woods," he said over his shoulder. "I couldn't have been more than ten, and I was practicing my bow-hunting skills on coons. He was maybe a year older than me. He'd never been to school a day in his life. First time I saw him, he just ran off. Melted into the woods. But then I saw him again, a few weeks later. I let him try my bow. Over time, we became . . . well, not friends—I don't think the Blakeneys have any friends—but acquaintances. I taught him a few things, brought him some books—he was a poor reader, but he had an eager mind—and he taught me more woodcraft than even my daddy knew." He shook his head. "One day, he brought me into the compound, introduced me to his people."

"What were they like?" Logan asked.

"I think it would be better if I let you make that judgment on your own. I'll wager you'll discover soon enough which of the legends are true—and which aren't."

"Are you saying there's some truth to the stories I heard in Pike Hollow?"

"Oh, there's some truth, all right—if we can convince the Blakeneys to reveal it."

The path was now hugging a steep rock face on one side and a narrow valley on the other. As best he could tell, Logan estimated they had walked about a mile, and the path was gradually trending eastward. Albright followed the invisible trail around a sharp bend in the cliff face, and suddenly Logan found himself confronted with another wall of endless twigs, lashed together with baling wire in vertical rows, seemingly as impenetrable as brick or concrete. This wall was shorter than the first he had encountered, however, and apparently less thick, and it disappeared into the surrounding forest on both sides almost immediately. There was no clearing before it, and the trees crowded in overhead; he could see nothing beyond the serried ranks of twigs, arranged so obsessively in their tightly fitted rows.

Albright stopped, turned to face Logan. "Listen carefully. I used to go inside fairly often as a kid. Since I've been back, I've only been inside two, maybe three times. If they do let us in, don't rile them up. Don't stare. Let me do the talking—until I turn it over to you. Follow my script, understand? And maybe—just maybe—you'll see some serious shit. Remember what I told you about the Adirondacks, and the Blakeneys in particular—there's history, and then there's mystery. Well, the mystery is what lies on the other side of *that*." And he jerked one thumb at the dense, ancient wall of twigs.

An old, empty drum of lubricating oil lay to one side, pitted and covered with rust. Picking up a stick, Albright hit the drum, first once, then a second time. And then he approached the wall.

"Nahum!" he called through the twigs, cupping his hands around his mouth. "Aaron! It's Albright. We need to talk."

No sound came from beyond the wall, except what sounded to Logan like the faint bleating of goats.

"Nahum!" Albright called again. "It's important."

A faint rustling noise from the far side. "Harrison?" came a hoarse, oddly accented voice.

"Yes, it's Harrison. We have to talk—about the police who are watching your place. Something's about to happen—something bad."

A pause.

"I've got someone with me. Maybe he can do something to stop it."

"What someone?" asked the voice from beyond the wall.

"His name's Logan. He's not from around these parts. And he's not here to judge you. He's here to help." And with this, Albright turned back and gave Logan a significant look.

For a moment, nothing happened. And then there was an audible stirring on the far side: a sliding, shifting sound, along with the creak of metal. Then a narrow opening appeared in the wall—an entrance so well disguised that Logan would never have known it was there. The doorlike structure pushed outward—and Logan came face-to-face with a gaunt man about six feet four, with long, unkempt hair, deeply set brown eyes, and a beard that reached down to his chest. His ragged clothes were a mass of patches and rude stitching. His huge hands were dirty and heavily callused from years of manual labor. He looked at Albright, then at Logan—his expression becoming suspicious—before turning back to Albright again.

"Harrison," he said.

"Nahum, we need to talk to your family—now. It's very important. *Vitally* important."

The man called Nahum scratched himself, seemed to ponder this a moment. Then wordlessly he stepped aside, allowing them admittance.

Logan ducked through the low enclosure—then stopped short, staring around in surprise.

30

In his travels as an enigmalogist, Logan had witnessed many strange things and exotic places: hidden tombs of Egyptian kings; the watery depths of Scottish lochs; the crumbling crypts of Romanian castles. But as he looked around, he had to stop and remind himself that he was standing on modern American soil. The Blakeney compound—at least, as much as he could see of it—looked like nothing so much as an ancient colony such as Jamestown or Plymouth. The site had been cut out of the living forest, and it used both impenetrable rocky cliff faces and the thick wall of twigs as protection from the outside world. He could see that the cleared area consisted of perhaps twenty-five acres or more. Dozens of buildings, some of them clearly a hundred or even two hundred years old, rose out of the grass. Many of them were crumbling, in the final stages of disrepair; others had been restored and expanded over time until they were rambling structures of the most bizarre architecture imaginable. Some of the buildings had tiled roofs; others were thatched or covered in wattle and daub. There was a smithy; a forge; what appeared to be a glassblowing apparatus; several barns; pens for poultry and livestock. Hogs wandered the area unvexed. Far ahead—toward the front of the property—were the outbuildings and fenced area for crops that he had spied on his first visit. There was no apparent order or planning to the community; it, along with the buildings it contained, appeared to simply have grown by accretion, making for confusion and a jumbled riot of workable, habitable, and barely habitable buildings. A few structures had in fact collapsed in on themselves and apparently been left to rot.

One building loomed over all—the vast, many-winged, gambrel-roofed structure whose upper stories he had previously seen from over the wall. It rose to his left, near the center of the cleared area, its back section close to the cliff face. It had been repaired, expanded, and remodeled so many times that it was impossible to guess its age or original design. One thing Logan was sure of: this sagging, lichen-encrusted building was the heart of the compound.

He had been staring, openmouthed. Now he realized that—silently, almost stealthily—a number of people had emerged from various places and approached them. They had formed a semi-circle before Logan and Albright, with the man named Nahum at their center. They all wore similar dress—rude homespun, patched and stitched to the last degree. Logan counted over a dozen. They were of all ages, from aged matriarchs to sturdy middle-aged men to an infant, sleeping in the arms of a young woman.

Recollecting himself, Logan tried to reach out to this ragtag assortment with his mind; tried to understand the emotions they were feeling. He sensed, not surprisingly, suspicion. He also sensed independence, fierce familial loyalty—and confusion. But he sensed no feelings of violence; none of the baby-stealing, backpacker-murdering emotions that, for example, were all too evidently possible in the mind of a Saul Woden. No: the overriding emotion Logan became aware of here . . . was *fear*.

Quickly, he assembled a mental picture of the group that stood before him: a close-knit, if admittedly uncouth and backward, extended family—one that had endured hostility and suspicion from the locals for so many years that they had grown extremely withdrawn. It was this, he expected, that had prompted their repulsion of his initial visit.

But what surprised him most—what he could not understand—was the strong, almost overpowering feeling of fear he sensed from the assemblage. Fear: and the unwelcome anticipation of some dread if familiar event that, it seemed, was about to happen.

Nahum turned to the assemblage and made a few hand gestures. Most of the crowd—after more furtive, curious looks at Logan—began to disperse, shuffling off in this or that direction, disappearing into dark doorways or headed toward the cultivated fields. Only Nahum and two men remained behind. The other two were older than Nahum, but whether they included his father, brothers, uncles, or some less savory combination, Logan could not imagine. What was clear was that these three constituted the elders of the community.

Now Nahum gestured to a fire pit some twenty yards away, surrounded by a series of long benches fashioned out of split logs. The three men started toward it, Albright and Logan following. The elders sat down on one of the log seats, while the visitors took seats across from them. The three elders conversed together a moment in low tones. And then Nahum—apparently the appointed spokesman—pointed to the man on his left, whose beard was even longer than his own. "Aaron," he said in his strange, rough accent. Then he pointed to the wizened, elderly figure seated on his right. "Esau."

Logan placed his hand on his own breast. "Jeremy. Jeremy Logan."

Albright spread his legs, placed his hands on his knees. "Nahum," he said, "we've been acquaintances of sorts, ever since we were young folk."

Nahum nodded.

"You know that I wouldn't lie to you, or do anything to harm you, or any of your kin."

Nahum nodded again.

"But the people of Pike Hollow feel differently. You know about the murders—and you can guess what the locals are saying about them."

Nahum did not answer, but his face darkened. The old man named Esau spat into the dirt.

"And now—well, a park ranger has been murdered. And that's changed everything. You've seen the police car parked at the end of your road?"

"We seen it," said the man named Aaron in a voice as deep as a gravel pit. "For days, they tried to get inside. Hollered, used them things—what, bullhorns. We ignored 'em."

"Well, when we went past about an hour ago, there was not one, but three cars. The head of the state troopers for these parts, a man named Krenshaw, aims to drive you out of here—one way or another. He's not one for half measures. I fear things may come to harm."

"What harm?" Nahum asked.

"I fear he'll burn you out, if necessary. You're the only suspects he's got—and the law's on his side."

Looks of shock, dismay, and anger came over the three men. Once more, they huddled together, whispering among themselves.

"But Jeremy Logan, here," Albright said, interrupting their confabulation, "he's got experience in these matters. He's seen a lot of unusual things in his time. He's a well-known, influential man—and it may be that he can stop this cop Krenshaw."

"How?" asked Nahum.

"I don't know that yet. Not exactly. But it might be he could stall him from acting. Or maybe—just maybe—point him toward the real killer."

All three men swiveled their eyes toward Logan.

"But you have to be honest with us. You have to answer a couple of questions."

Another huddled murmuring. Then Nahum looked back at them. "What you want to know?"

"Tell us about the doctor. The old man."

For a moment, the three men went still. "The . . . scientist fellow?" Nahum said. "The one with the white hair?"

"Yes. He came here, didn't he?"

It took Nahum a moment to answer. "Yes."

"How many times did he come?"

This time, it took Nahum even longer. "Twice."

"And he asked a lot of questions. About your history. And about your clan. No doubt he'd been to Pike Hollow, heard the rumors." He paused. "Why did you let him in? Agree to talk with him?"

"We needed money," Aaron interjected. "For medicine. Penicillin. Rebekah had the chest fever awful bad. No poultice would help."

"And Feverbridge—the scientist—offered you money."

More nods.

"But he wanted something in return for the money—didn't he? More than just history."

The three remained silent.

"Didn't he?" Albright pressed.

Finally, Nahum nodded reluctantly.

"What was it?"

For a moment, nobody moved. Then Nahum pantomimed the act of swabbing the inside of his mouth with a Q-tip.

"A DNA sample," Logan murmured. Then, aloud: "Who among you did he swab?"

"Me," said Nahum. "Esau. Ruth."

"But those weren't all, were they?" Albright asked. "Because by this time, you'd told him of the other. Right? After all, you needed the money—and Dr. Feverbridge, who no doubt had heard the rumors coming out of Pike Hollow, knew how to get information out of you."

"No," Nahum said, shaking his head.

"Oh, yes," Albright pressed. "He wanted a swab from Zephraim, as well."

The three elders exchanged glances. Watching, Logan sensed a sharp increase in both their fear and their reluctance to speak further.

"And you let him have it. You needed the money too badly to refuse. And he promised not to tell anyone."

Nahum hung his head. After a moment, he nodded. "Didn't hurt nobody. He said it was just for a test, like."

"Who is Zephraim?" Logan whispered to Albright.

Albright leaned in toward him. "He's the reason the Blakeneys are so afraid of the Pike Hollow locals—and why they won't let any strangers inside their compound."

Now Logan spoke up. "I need to meet Zephraim."

Real alarm flashed between the three men across the fire pit. "No," Nahum said. "You cain't."

"Why not?"

"You just cain't," came the evasive answer.

"Tell him why," Albright said in a quiet voice. "Tell him the real reason."

Nahum began to speak; hesitated. Then he pointed to the sky, which was just beginning to darken.

"'Cause it's the changing time," he said.

Albright sat forward on the log. "Listen to me," he addressed the three. "I told you: Jeremy here has seen a lot of strange things. He's not going to judge you—and he's not going to judge Zephraim. Understand, we can't make any guarantees. But if he is to have any chance at all of helping you, he has to see everything. And that means Zephraim."

The three elders conversed nervously among themselves.

"It's either that or the state police," Albright said.

The whispered conversation went on for another moment. Then, with a kind of weariness that had nothing physical about it, Nahum pushed himself up from the log. The other two Blakeneys followed suit.

"This way," Nahum said.

Logan and Albright swung in behind the three elders as they began following a muddy path between dairies, a candlery, and, farther along, what looked like some kind of shed for repairing machinery. There was apparently no electricity in the compound, and candles and kerosene torches began to appear in the passing windows. Logan glanced at his watch: it was five thirty.

"Nahum told me about Zephraim, once or twice, back when we were kids," Albright said to Logan in a low voice. "He was still a young child—I only got glimpses of him now and then. I haven't heard a word about him since I returned from downstate. But look how twitchy the whole clan is—they're not usually the nervous type; they've been estranged from the local populace far too long for that. No: Zephraim's at the bottom of this, you can bet that much. God only knows what Feverbridge got up to, exactly, before he fell off that cliff."

As they continued to climb the path, it became increasingly clear that their destination was the huge structure that towered over the entire compound. On closer inspection it was an even more bizarre building than it first appeared. It seemed to have been originally made of mud brick, but its exterior walls were covered over with so many layers of clapboard, homemade stucco, and scavenged concrete chunks of assorted sizes and shapes that it was impossible to be sure. Logan judged it to be five or maybe six stories in height, but the mismatched gables and dormers that sprouted from the main structure and its various dependencies had so little in common with their brethren, and the numerous windows—some made of ancient glass of circular pattern, others with rude blinds covering them, others simply oiled paper hammered into place—were at so many different levels that they presented only confusion to the eye.

Nahum led the way inside. Logan had expected to find a parlor, or living room, or greeting area of some sort, but saw nothing more than a narrow, low-ceilinged hallway burrowing back into untold distances. The walls were made of wide, rough-hewn beams. While it had been growing increasingly dark outside, once

the elders shut the front door behind them Logan found himself in almost total blackness. A match flared; guttering tapers
suddenly flickered in wall sconces; a kerosene torch was lit; and
Nahum gestured them to follow him along a circuitous path that
led up creaking stairs, along passages, down short flights, and up
still longer ones, passing innumerable doors, most closed, a few
open onto scenes of almost indescribable rustication. Logan soon
lost all sense of his bearings, or just how many stories they had
climbed. An audible gust of wind shook the structure, causing it
to shudder unnervingly. And still they climbed.

And then, quite suddenly, the stairs ended at a small landing
before a single wooden door. It was bound by two stout bands of
iron, and instead of a doorknob it was secured by a padlock. The
group gathered together on the landing, huddled close together in
the confined space. Nahum set the torch on a table, then rapped
on the door.

There was no response. Logan imagined he could hear a low,
scuttling noise beyond.

Nahum knocked again. When there was still no reply, he bent
over, lips near the padlock.

"Zephraim?" he said in a calm, soothing voice, the way one
might talk to an animal. "Zephraim, it's Nahum. I'm coming in
now."

31

Nahum undid the padlock, opened the door slightly—gingerly—then pushed it wide. Ahead lay a darkened space. He stepped inside, followed by the others.

Logan found himself in a small garret room. There was no furniture save for a simple, crudely constructed table, holding a clay pitcher of water and a wooden bowl containing what looked like gruel, and a three-legged stool perched in the center of the floor. A single window, barred on the inside with several pieces of wood, admitted just the faintest traces of afterglow from the dying sun. He realized that he must be in the top room of the structure: the one he'd seen from outside the wall, the first time he had tried to visit the compound. The only real light came from the lantern, sitting on the table outside the door.

The three elders arranged themselves against one wall, and Logan and Albright followed suit. The wall, he noticed, was not the rough wooden planks he had seen in the rest of the building, but covered in some kind of cotton batting, greasy and torn, stuffing protruding from a hundred tears.

Seated on the three-legged stool was a man about forty years old, tall and muscular. He was dressed in the same homespun as the others, the only difference being that, instead of wearing trousers and a work shirt, he was dressed in something more closely resembling the loose vestments of a monk. He had a rough beard, like the others, and his brown hair fell in uncombed knots and tangles to his shoulders. He glanced at the elders without interest as they took their places against the wall. When his eyes reached Albright, curiosity and recognition flared briefly across his face before fading again. Finally, he saw Logan: and fear abruptly flooded over his features.

"No!" he said, pointing at Logan. "Make him go!"

"He's here to help, Zephraim," Nahum said in the same soothing voice he'd used before.

"He'll tell! He'll be telling them others!"

"No, he won't. You remember Harrison, here—you met him as a sprat. He's done staked his word on this man. And that scientist fellow who came—he never told a living soul about you, now, did he? And that was, oh, eight, nine months back."

Zephraim looked at Logan with what the enigmalogist sensed was a confused welter of emotions—suspicion, uncertainty, fear, maybe a faint stirring of hope. "How can he help?" he said finally in a despairing voice, turning away from them.

"Don't know, exactly. Not sure he done, neither. But they want to watch your turning."

"No!" Zephraim said, wheeling back again. "It's not for others to see! I don't—"

But the man stopped in mid-sentence and looked away. Logan saw he was suddenly staring at the boarded-up window. It was no longer afterglow that streamed through the cracks between the boards—now it was moonlight.

The three elders exchanged glances but said nothing more. The air in the room became strangely charged, as if with electricity. It seemed everyone there was waiting for something to happen.

Which, Logan realized, was precisely the case.

Zephraim remained motionless, staring at the boarded window, for perhaps fifteen minutes. During that time, the moonbeams grew a little stronger, gilding the rough edges of the wood with a pale, ethereal hue. Logan was reminded of the color he'd seen re-created in Feverbridge's secret lab.

Now Zephraim abruptly stood up. He began to move restlessly around the little room: picking up the bowl of gruel, then replacing it; pacing while muttering under his breath. Then, one by one, he stopped at the five men lined up against the far wall, looking intently at them in turn. Lastly he came to Logan, stared hard into his eyes. Zephraim's own eyes had turned red-rimmed, bloodshot. Almost unwillingly, Logan allowed his empathetic senses to reach out to the man. He still sensed suspicion and uncertainty. But the fear was now gone. And there was something else: while he sensed the strangeness, the unnaturalness, he'd felt the first time he stood outside the walled compound, he felt none of the terrible *wrongness* of the two murder sites he had witnessed.

Zephraim turned away and, pacing again, resumed his low muttering. It might have been a trick of the light, but the man's skin seemed to take on a darker, rougher cast. "Close the door," he said roughly.

Nobody moved.

"Close the door!" he almost barked.

After a moment, Esau moved toward the door. He did so with the reluctant but familiar motion of someone who had done this countless times before. When the door closed, shutting out the light from the landing, the room immediately grew dim. And yet not as dim as Logan might have expected: light from the second night of the full moon seeped strongly between the cracks of the boarded-up window.

And now a change came over Zephraim. Several hives, or weals, began breaking out over his skin—large, irregularly shaped, almost black with subcutaneous blood. A low rattle began to sound in his throat. He moved back and forth irregularly, once, twice, all the time shaking his head so that his hair flew like a dark corona around him. It must have been a trick of the light, but the man's beard, the hair on his arms, seemed to grow thicker and more rough; the nails of his hands appeared to lengthen and spread. The three elders exchanged glances once more.

Zephraim growled. And then—with a single, animal-like bound—he leapt for the window.

"Zephraim!" cried Nahum. "No—!"

But it was too late: with several violent, powerful yanks, Zephraim pulled the wooden planks away from the window with a harsh splintering sound. The light of the full moon streamed in, unimpeded. And then, quite suddenly, Zephraim seemed to go mad: he began rushing back and forth, growling; running to the window and throwing his face outward, baying to the moonlight; then, turning away, he ran around the room, falling onto all fours before rising to his feet again, overturning the stool, picking up the clay jug of water and dashing it to the ground, where it broke in a million pieces.

Immediately, the elders turned and made for the door. With

both hands, Nahum took Albright and Logan by their elbows and propelled them out onto the landing, where he turned back, closed the door, and padlocked it.

"What just happened?" Logan said, shocked by what he had just witnessed, unlike anything in his long experience.

"I warned you," Nahum replied. "It's the changing time. The moon-sickness—it's strong in him."

Beyond the door, the sound of crashing and baying continued unabated.

"How long will it last?" Albright asked.

"'Til moonfall."

"And is he a danger to others until then?" Logan asked.

"No," Nahum said. "Not to others."

And—looking into the man's eyes—Logan suddenly understood. The lock on the door, the unusual padding on the walls of the garret room: they were not there to protect others from Zephraim . . . but to protect him from himself.

32

The group made the long trip back down through the rambling house in silence. Gradually, the sounds from behind the locked door grew more remote. Exiting the building, the five returned to the fire pit and sat down once again. Here, Logan could once again hear, faintly, Zephraim's growling and baying, through the boarded window that he had torn open.

The three elders looked at each other, then at Logan and Albright. They seemed both abashed and relieved—abashed at the display of such a strange and embarrassing phenomenon; relieved that the display was over.

"This 'moon-sickness' Zephraim suffers from," Logan asked. "It runs in your family, doesn't it?"

Nahum nodded. "From what my grandpappy told me, there's

always been one or two of the clan been touched, more or less. But none like Zephraim."

So with Zephraim, the syndrome—or condition—has found full flower. Logan thought of what Fred the bartender had said of the Blakeneys: his reference to "tainted blood." "What form does it usually take, then?"

Nahum thought a moment. "Folks get agitated. Skin turns dark in spots. Boils come out, like them you saw on Zephraim."

"And you say it lasts until the moon goes down?"

Nahum nodded.

"But only during a full moon—right?"

"That's right."

So it was the intensity of the moonlight, the light of the full moon, that was necessary to trigger the effect. In that way, it was not unlike the experiment with the shrews that Feverbridge had demonstrated to him.

"What if it's a cloudy or a rainy night?" Albright asked. "If the moon is obscured, say?"

"Nothing happens," said Aaron.

Logan thought for a minute. "The effects sound uncomfortable. Zephraim certainly seemed to be suffering from them. And yet he sought out the moonlight—he ripped the boards off the window. Why?"

"Don't rightly know," Nahum said. "Zephraim, he don't like to talk about it much. Best as I can make out, you're drawn to it—drawn despite yourself. It's a craving, like. And . . . I think it gives a feeling of—well, some kind of power."

"Like a wolf," Albright said.

Nahum nodded. His eyes had been cast downward, but now he looked up, directly at Logan, and the moonlight reflected brightly on the corneas. "But no matter how bad he gits, he never hurts anyone. He never gits violent."

The other two nodded vigorously.

"Has anybody but us ever seen the . . . the changing time?" Albright asked. "Besides Dr. Feverbridge, I mean?"

"Many years back," said the patriarch, Esau. "Uncle Levi, he used to get the moon-sickness pretty bad. One time he done scaled the wall. I think one or two folks from Pike Hollow saw him running toward the woods."

Logan and Albright exchanged glances. That, perhaps, explained where the rumors came from.

"Ever since," Esau went on, "we've always kept kinfolk with the moon-sickness locked up on full moon nights."

"Dr. Feverbridge," Logan said, turning to Nahum. "Did he want anything else from Zephraim—other than the swab from his cheek, I mean?"

Nahum hesitated once again. "Yes. He wanted . . ." He pantomimed drawing blood from the cubital vein. "Paid us two hundred fifty dollar to do it. I done told you—Rebekah had the chest fever real bad." He repeated this as if to explain away a lingering guilt.

"I understand," Logan said. He was still trying to process what he had just witnessed in the garret room: the bizarre transformation—no other word was sufficient—of Zephraim Blakeney. It was like the change the short-tailed shrews had exhibited: except this went beyond mere behavior; there were actual morphological changes, subtle but undeniable. Although he had no idea of what, exactly, the underlying biologic cause was, it was evident there was a genetic trait in the Blakeney clan—perhaps because of inbreeding, perhaps just due to a fluke in their particular genome—that rendered them hypersensitive to moon-light. And Zephraim was the most sensitive of all. No wonder Dr. Feverbridge had sought him out, paid handsomely for samples of blood and DNA. It seemed to dovetail with the lines of research mentioned in both articles Logan had seen on Jessup's computer screen: the re-creation of moonlight *and* morphological change.

He realized Nahum was asking him a question and, with effort, pushed these speculations aside. "I'm sorry?"

"I said: can you help us?"

Logan took a deep breath. "I'm not sure. I hope so. I'll do my best. There are a few things I need to look into—and the sooner the better."

The group fell silent. Zephraim's distant howlings became audible once again. The three elders shifted on the rough wooden seat, clearly agitated.

"I have one last question," Logan said. "Ever since I entered your compound, I've sensed fear—fear from all of you. What, exactly, is it that you're afraid of?"

The three looked at him in disbelief. "What you think, mister?" Nahum said. "If there's some monster out there—something killing people, tearing 'em up—don't you think *we* feared of it, too?"

"And with the moon-sickness running in our kinfolk," Aaron said, "that critter just might try and seek us out on purpose."

"That's enough to frighten anybody," said Albright. "And if that wasn't sufficient, there's the hatred and distrust of all the locals—not to mention the plans Krenshaw is putting together." He stood up. "Thank you all—for letting us on your land, for trusting us . . . and for letting us see Zephraim. We'll be going now."

They walked back down the path to the massive wall of twigs.

Nahum undid a spool of coiled wire, opened the carefully hidden door, then nodded solemnly to both of them in turn. They ducked out through the opening and the door was immediately closed behind them. With no light at all now save for that of the full moon, filtering down through the branches, the surrounding forest was a woven braid of almost unrelieved black. Albright reached into his pocket, pulled out a flashlight, and turned it on.

"Do you really think you're going to be able to follow that path?" Logan asked. "Even with a flashlight? I could barely make it out in daylight."

"Are you trying to be insulting?" Albright replied. "That's the second time today you've questioned my woodcraft. Watch this." He snapped off the light and returned it to his pocket. "I'll take us back to the road using nothing but the moonlight. Not as impressive perhaps as what you just witnessed in there, but I think it'll stop you from asking a third time. Put your hand on my shoulder now—wouldn't want you getting lost. And for God's sake, move as quietly as you can: it's a full moon, remember, and whatever killed Jessup and the others is out there—somewhere."

33

They walked all the way back to Albright's pickup and drove the short distance down 3A to his house, without speaking. When Albright got out, Logan did the same, automatically following him inside.

"Well, what do you think?" Albright said, breaking the silence at last. "I'll bet even you've never seen anything like *that* before. I know I haven't."

Logan just shook his head. "I guess I've got some work to do."

"Well, I suggest that you hurry it up." Albright took the rifle off the wall, grabbed a box of bullets from the mantelpiece, and loaded it. Then he leaned the rifle up against the fireplace. "Because tomorrow's the last night of the full moon—and it sounds like our friend Krenshaw has a real hard-on to prosecute some, ah, justice."

Logan thanked him for his time and effort, then left the house and drove back to his own cabin at Cloudwater. He had a great deal to think about—and not much time to do it in.

First, he accessed the Internet and looked into possible inherited conditions that might explain what was afflicting Zephraim. The darkening of the skin, he suspected, might be connected to melanin—perhaps a hyperpigmentation of brown eumelanin that was—bizarrely—produced by reflected moonlight instead of direct sunlight. If this was the case, then the phenomenon of photoprotection—suites of molecular mechanisms designed to protect humans from damaging sunlight—might be working in reverse, so to speak, endowing him with actual physical *benefits* from the moon's beams. If a sudden and dramatic spike in melanin production was responsible, then neuromelanin—a strange and little-understood polymer that was found in the brain—might also be responsible for his marked change in behavior, especially if it could be linked to a spike in the secretion of a hormone like adrenaline.

Along the same lines, the distended nails that Logan had thought he'd seen emerge from the ends of Zephraim's fingers could be attributed to hyperkeratosis—which, since it was also known to produce skin irritations such as acne and keratosis pilaris, could account for the weals he'd seen appear on Zephraim's skin.

And then of course there was Ambras syndrome, or hypertrichosis—the "werewolf syndrome"—that caused abnormal hair growth over the entire body. The bearded ladies of the freak shows of elder days were frequently sufferers of this affliction.

Hyperpigmentation, hyperkeratosis, hypertrichosis—all these could potentially be behind, scientifically, what he had seen in the garret room of the Blakeney residence. But they could not explain the rapid onset with which all three manifested themselves—nor could they explain how, presumably, they all disappeared with the same alacrity once the moon went down. And, of course, there was no record in the online medical and scientific journals that Logan consulted of any of these conditions being brought on by moonlight.

Was it possible that what Zephraim—and certain others in his clan, to a lesser degree—was suffering from was some genetic abnormality, or perhaps some syndrome, as yet unknown to science? Sudden hair growth, increased physical ability, long nails, darkened skin (which only made the additional hair appear that much more dramatic)—these all sounded like the historical werewolf sightings, recounted over the centuries, that he'd read by the dozens, although—as usual with hysterical observations— exaggerated by fear and ignorance. There was one difference, however—in Zephraim's case, while there might be certain physical changes . . . there was no bloodlust, no furious spasms of violence.

At least, so the Blakeneys had told him. And the fear they'd exhibited; the way they had locked Zephraim up for his own protection—and, most of all, the feelings he had sensed from Zephraim after the change—convinced Logan they were telling the truth.

Then there was something else—something Logan found himself almost unwilling to confront. And that was Chase Feverbridge. Feverbridge had learned about Zephraim, and about the unique "moon-sickness" that the Blakeney clan suffered from. He'd taken DNA and blood samples. But none of this had come up in his demonstration to Logan, that night in the secret lab behind the fire station. That demonstration had focused on how moonlight—pure moonlight, filtered through the dust of the moon's atmosphere but unhindered by the pollution that now surrounded the earth—could cause behavioral modifications. Feverbridge's words came back to him: *Was it possible this unusual quality of light, when viewed by diurnal creatures on earth, could affect the brain sufficiently to cause changes in behavior? And could the full moon alone be enough to achieve that? That was the beginnings of a working hypothesis: that the effect of this special, polarized moonlight, entering the brain, could cause an unusual response: fear, excitability, aggression.*

Feverbridge had demonstrated—and Logan had seen—the results for himself. But those results, though dramatic, had all been behavioral—as posited in the first article he'd read on Jessup's computer. What he'd just witnessed happen to Zephraim had been not only behavioral, but morphological. Albeit temporarily, albeit only to a relatively small degree, Zephraim had *physically changed.*

Yet this had not made up any part of the experiment Logan had seen in the secret lab, although it had perhaps been hinted at in the second, final article he'd read on Jessup's computer, published eight or nine months earlier. There were any number of possible reasons for this omission. Perhaps Feverbridge had been unable to make any viable use of Zephraim's DNA. He had hoped to— hence the optimistic article—but ultimately it had proven impossible. It was quite possible the Blakeneys manifested a genetic trait that was simply too unusual or exotic to be manipulated in a laboratory . . . and so Feverbridge had fallen back to his original research.

Another possibility was that he had not mentioned the

Blakeneys to Logan because he'd promised to keep their secret. After all, Logan had made the same sort of promise—the old scientist would not be likely to betray a confidence like that.

And yet, there was one other scenario running through the back of Logan's mind—one that he did not wish to pursue. And it had to do with the dog run he'd seen while visiting Laura Feverbridge.

With a sigh, he closed the lid of his laptop. Lack of sleep made him feel almost stuporous—and it was now past three in the morning. Whatever the explanation might be, in Zephraim Blakeney, Logan had found someone consummately worthy of further study: an enigmalogist's dream. And not just for the rare enigmalogist like himself. There were roughly forty thousand identified diseases currently in the world. It was, perversely perhaps, the dream of every medical practitioner, from clinician to biophysicist, to discover yet another. Perhaps he had done that. But that study, whatever form it might take, if any, would have to wait. Because there were other, darker forces at work: forces that had to be tackled first. Whatever Zephraim actually was—whether or not he was the werewolf of legend—there was something far more murderous on the loose. The moon was still full—and that meant he had a ticking clock.

Leaning back in his chair, he closed his eyes, mentally trying to sort out all the pieces to this strange puzzle. The speculation of the residents of Pike Hollow. The concerns of his friend Jessup—first mere uncertainty; later, apparently, suspicion. The transformation of Zephraim, and the clan's "moon-sickness"—something he'd witnessed with his own eyes. The final articles that Dr. Feverbridge had written, and the experiment he'd demonstrated to Logan in the secret lab. Somewhere, hidden among all these strands, was the thread that would lead to the answer. . . .

He was roused by a light rap on his door. He moved in his chair, blinked in surprise at the bright sunlight flooding his cabin. Glancing at his watch, he saw with disbelief that it was past one p.m. He had fallen asleep and slept straight through the morning, waking only as his lunch was being left outside his front door.

His limbs ached from hours spent sleeping in a chair, but he could not wait. He ran into the bathroom, washed his face and hands, poured cold water over his head to sharpen his senses. Grabbing a comb, he ran it through his hair. And then, picking up his cell phone, car keys—and a flashlight—he ran out the front door and down the dirt path that led to the lot where his rented Jeep was parked.

34

It was nearly half past three when Logan pulled into the driveway of the converted fire station. He paused at the mouth of the driveway to make a brief call, then continued down to the parking area. As he got out of the Jeep, he saw Laura Feverbridge come out of the residence building and walk in the direction of the lab. When she saw him, she stopped and smiled.

"Jeremy," she said. "What a nice surprise."

"Nice to see you as well," he said. "I wish it was under better circumstances."

When he said this, her smile faded. "Yes. I heard about Jessup. What a terrible thing. I met him twice—he seemed like such a nice man." She nodded ahead. "Come on, we can talk in the lab."

As they walked, Logan realized that something was different.

Then he realized what it was: there was no barking of dogs, no eager frisking about their heels. He glanced in the direction of the dog run, saw that it was empty.

"Where are Toshi and Mischa?" he asked.

Laura's look grew still more troubled. "They ran away."

"What? Both of them?"

"As far as I can tell. You remember how agitated they were becoming—I had to lock them in the dog run at night. Then, two mornings ago, I let them out as usual, went to get their breakfasts . . . and when I returned they were gone. I spent half the morning combing the surrounding woods, calling and whistling. Nothing."

They stepped inside the lab and took a seat at one of the tables. "How's your father?" Logan asked.

"Busier than ever. It's like I told you—he seems to have found a new life."

Logan glanced around at the lab tables; the scientific equipment; the animal cages. He sensed a false brightness coming from the naturalist's daughter. "Did Pace go into town?"

"No. He's out searching for the dogs."

When Logan looked at her silently for a long moment, Laura lowered her eyes. "Actually, that's not true. Kevin's left us."

"When?"

"Just yesterday afternoon. Packed up and took a taxi into Lake Placid, without a word of warning."

"Why, exactly?"

"Why not?" Laura shrugged. "The isolation, Mark's death, the dogs running away—but I think it was the killing of the ranger that was the final straw." She glanced at him. "Was it . . . as bad as the others?"

"Worse."

She shuddered. "Still no suspects?"

"Well, there's a paroled killer named Saul Woden the authorities were keeping their eyes on. However, he has a foolproof alibi for when Randall Jessup was killed. Now the suspicions of the state police have shifted to the Blakeney clan—and shifted strongly, I might add."

Laura shook her head. "Typical backwoods prejudice. Oh, I've no doubt the Blakeneys are an inbred, reclusive, perhaps illiterate family. So I've always heard, anyway. Such things aren't their fault—it's a product of the environment in which they've always lived. But naturally, I suppose it would make them a target of suspicion—especially for the ignorant."

There was a brief silence. "Laura," Logan said at last in a gentle voice. "I'm sorry to have to say this. But the first time you and I spoke, you professed never to have heard of the Blakeneys."

Laura flushed red. She turned away.

"Jeremy—" she began.

"No," he interrupted. "I think it would be easier if I did the talking."

After a moment, still turned away from him, she nodded.

"I have a theory. Not all the pieces are there—not necessarily— but I think most of them are. You see, I read your father's last two articles: the ones you said subjected him to even more severe ridicule from the scientific community than before. One speculated on ways the moon's atmosphere could be responsible for the lunar effect: something your father demonstrated to me most convincingly. The other—the last and in some ways more pertinent paper—spoke of transformational biology—in effect, metamorphosis—and how animal DNA could perhaps precipitate the mutation of human DNA. I also know that your father visited the Blakeney clan—and in exchange for money, obtained DNA swabs and, in the case of Zephraim Blakeney, plasma. Zephraim Blakeney, who suffers from some genetic affliction that causes actual, if temporary, physical changes in the presence of strong moonlight: the light of the full moon."

Laura remained silent, facing away from Logan, as he spoke.

"Your father was convinced—rightly so—about the veracity of his hypothesis on the moon's atmosphere—specifically, the composition of lunar dust—precipitating the lunar effect on earth. But now, burning with rage at the way his work had been spurned and scorned—and perhaps witnessing Zephraim's 'moon-sickness' with his own eyes, as I did just last night—I think your father revised the theories he put forward in his second paper. Instead of animal DNA influencing human DNA, *human* DNA—in particular, that of Zephraim Blakeney—could influence *animal* DNA."

He paused. Laura remained silent.

"Your father is a skilled biochemist as well as a naturalist—you told me so yourself. That secret lab of yours is filled with equipment more suited to a medical or biology lab than it is that of a naturalist. It's not much of a leap to assume that—using Zephraim's DNA, in concert with the developments he'd already made on his own—your father synthesized a serum to cause just such a transformation. And since the serum was dependent on Zephraim's condition, it would only manifest itself during the full moon. I would imagine that, human DNA being so different from that of small animals like the ones you keep in these labs, the serum would be incompatible with them—it would either have no effect, or it might kill. Your father could reproduce behavioral changes in shrews and mice, via artificial moonlight, but not morphological ones—a larger creature would be necessary for that. And that is why he ultimately tried the serum *on his own two dogs*."

Logan stood up and began pacing the lab. "It makes perfect sense. That's why the dogs were acting strangely when I saw them last, just after the full moon had passed its cycle. And that's why they're missing now—during the full moon. Right? For whatever reason—perhaps some artifact overlooked in the DNA resequencing—he added not only superior strength and abilities to those animals . . . but uncontrollable violence, as well. Violence *not* present in Zephraim or his kin. Is this the result of confronting nature, Laura—of trying to play God? In a desperate attempt to prove his theories, your father unwittingly created two monsters, monsters he couldn't control without risking his life and yours . . . and they have now been unleashed upon the world. And killed four people."

Now, finally, Laura turned to face him. And the expression on her face stopped him in mid-stride.

"You're very clever, Jeremy," she said in a quiet voice. "And you're very good at what you do. It's true, what you say—at least, most of it: the synthesis of the serum, the use of it on a control subject. In fact, you're right about almost everything . . . except for one item, one very important item. The fact is, all this time you've been going down the right road, looking in the right direction—but all that same time, the final piece, the piece you've missed, has been staring you in the face. You just haven't seen it yet."

Logan looked into the unreadable expression in Laura Feverbridge's eyes. And then all at once—with a stunning, terrible moment of revelation—he understood.

35

"Your father," Logan breathed. "He used it on himself."

"Who else?" Laura replied. "Do you think he would let any other living being but himself be the guinea pig? His daughter? His *dogs*?"

Logan nodded slowly. In retrospect, it made perfect sense. Feverbridge had been a ticking clock. The academic slights and humiliations he'd suffered had caused him to attempt suicide—was using the experimental serum on himself such a leap? Hardly: he was clearly obsessed enough to do so. And if it had succeeded on a human—if he had been able to conclusively demonstrate physical changes caused by the full moon—his disgrace would have been turned to immediate success.

But something had gone wrong—terribly wrong.

"Tell me what happened," he said.

She took a deep, shuddering breath. "I hadn't known he was going to do it until it was too late. He had already worked out how to employ certain metamorphosing qualities of caterpillars—using human analogues of imaginal discs would be necessary for the incredibly rapid cell division required for the transformation he wanted. Once he'd acquired the DNA of Zephraim Blakeney, who obviously demonstrated morphological changes under the influence of the full moon, he combined it with his research on imaginal discs. Then he resequenced this into a formula that could be administered to a human. Just as Zephraim returned to his normal self after moonfall, he assumed that he would, as well. But as a safeguard, he built a kind of 'memory' into the imaginal discs—a protein that would denature after a certain number of hours—to ensure that the transformation was temporary. He ran an exhaustive battery of tests and simulations. And then he—he injected himself with it."

She took another breath. "It was only then that he summoned me to watch his triumph. And his theory proved correct . . . only too correct. It was the second night of a full moon. And as we sat there—the others had gone to bed—he began to change. Except it was not what he'd expected. He anticipated minor morphological developments: skin discoloration, hair growth, various systemic changes. And sure enough, once the moonlight hit him, they began. But he hadn't counted on the side effects."

"What were they?" Logan urged.

"Difficult to describe. We're still trying to reverse them, even now. As best we can tell, the metamorphosing 'boost' of the DNA resequencing made the effect far more pronounced in him than it was in Zephraim Blakeney. It was . . . it was frightening." She looked up suddenly at Logan. "Can you believe that I, his daughter, could say such a thing? But it's true, and there's no other way to describe it: the transformation was fearful. And worst of all, the resequencing had—as you just speculated—made him suscep- tible to the lunar effect. It made him aggressive, even violent—like the shrews you saw in the demonstration a few weeks ago. He dashed out of the laboratory . . . and into the night."

She lapsed into silence. Logan glanced at his watch: four thirty. He waited for her to begin again.

"He encountered the old backpacker I told you about. The man's reaction to his appearance, the startled cries, enraged my father. He threw him off the cliff. Somehow, the sudden, unex- pected violence of that response seemed to bring him around. He came back to the lab, told me what he'd done."

She was still looking directly at Logan. "So you see, my father *did* have to die—just not for the reason I told you. We had to hide him away, work someplace on our own until we could find a way to reverse the effects of his serum. Because the safeguard he'd introduced—the 'memory' of the imaginal discs—did not func- tion as expected. The transformative ability remained active— and the next night, it happened again. This time, we locked him away in the building that would later become our secret lab. The next morning, I hiked out to the backpacker's body. Just as I described to you, I swapped his possessions for my father's. Then I installed my father in the lab, ordered the equipment we would need. I waited a day before reporting him missing. I almost hoped that Mark would discover the body on one of his hikes. But he didn't—and so I went to the police."

She sighed. "And ever since, we've been looking for an anti- dote, so to speak—a way to reverse the process he initiated. We had some immediate success: we were able to roll back the influence of the lunar effect so that he no longer felt any violent tendencies.

But the . . . physical transformations continue to occur with every full moon. My father works on the problem every day, in our outpost in the woods. And at night, I've gone to help, too—except on the nights of the full moon. On those nights, he always retreats to his private lab, the one behind the door in the far wall. He is too ashamed . . . he won't let me look at him. I think he saw the horror in my face the first times he changed—and it's too painful for him to see that again."

"So he locks himself in his private lab," Logan said. "A lab within a lab, which you can never enter."

"Yes. It has only a single window, covered with tar paper. It doesn't compensate for the effects of the full moon—not completely—but it helps. I . . . I never go near the lab on those nights. I stay away, let him keep his dignity."

"And you're sure he remains in that private lab as long as the full moon is out?"

"Of course. He can't bear for anyone to see him when he's in that—that state. Besides, we can't take the chance he might encounter that vicious beast out roaming the forest."

"You mean the rogue bear," Logan said. "Or rogue wolf."

All at once, she caught the insinuation. "Oh, you're wrong—you're wrong! He hates what's happened to him, what he's done to himself—all he wants to do is lock himself away until it passes. Besides, I told you, we managed to cancel out the violent manifestations, such as they were—and in any case they were never anything, *anything* like what happened to those four poor men. It was a sudden spasm of anger, never to be repeated and always to be regretted."

She lapsed into silence. It was several minutes before Logan spoke again.

"Laura . . ." he began. "I don't know what to say. This is

all so shocking. What you've described happening to your father is . . . remarkable. Also unfortunate, to say the least—in that it did not work as planned. And I appreciate the fact you've been working day and night to try to reverse it. But it was bad enough when you substituted your father's identity for that lone hiker's. This is far worse. You're hiding—harboring—a killer."

"He didn't mean to do it, Jeremy . . ." Laura said, almost pleading. "He wasn't himself, it was a terrible mistake. The father I know would never want to hurt anybody. Don't you see that?"

"Yes, I do see that. But it doesn't change what he did. When the authorities learn of the circumstances, they'll—"

"They'll put him in a lab and examine him. Like a zoo animal. Or a freak. And that will be the death of him . . . or maybe, worse than death."

"No. I won't let that happen—I promise. But he has to be taken to a facility where he can be helped."

She merely hung her head, saying nothing.

"Laura—let me talk to him."

At this, she looked up. "No! Moonrise is too near. He'll have locked himself in his private lab by now."

"Then I'll talk to him through the door."

"You can't, he won't—"

"Laura, *please*. You've worked on the problem for six months now, without success. This is the best chance that I—that *we*—have to help him."

She sat motionless for several minutes. And then—without looking at him—she rose and led the way out of the primary lab and into the woods.

36

As they approached the lab, hidden deep in the woods, the sun was close to setting behind the horizon. A few stray clouds hung in the sky.

The building was dark, apparently deserted. Laura stepped up to the door, hesitated. Logan took hold of her shoulder, gave it a brief squeeze. After a moment, she turned the knob and opened the door.

No lights were on inside, and Laura snapped on the bank of switches. The lab was as Logan remembered it, with its microscopes and DNA sequencer, a host of other equipment and instrumentation, the animal cages—and the door in the far wall, which was currently closed.

Moving slowly, hesitatingly, Laura approached that door.

"Father?" she said after a moment in a voice both anxious and hopeful.

There was no response from the far side.

"Father, please answer."

Now Logan heard a stirring beyond the door. "Laura, we had an agreement. You must leave me alone on the nights of the full moon. You know I can't bear for you to see me like this."

"I have Jeremy Logan with me," she said.

Feverbridge did not respond.

"Father—he knows everything."

Another moment of silence. And then the door slowly opened and a dark figure appeared in the doorway. As it emerged into the light, Logan made out Chase Feverbridge. He was dressed, not in a lab coat, but in torn old trousers and a loose-fitting shirt of rough wool. He seemed even taller than Logan remembered, and as he looked from Logan to his own daughter, a strange light shone in his eyes. Over his shoulder, Logan could see the cot in the small back room. This time he could also make out the tar-paper-covered window, a large sink, and a bank of instrumentation, but precisely what its purpose was he could not discern in the dimness.

"What does he know, exactly?" the naturalist asked.

"He's been to the Blakeney compound. He's seen Zephraim's transformation—and he knows about the DNA and plasma samples you took from him."

"You told him?" Feverbridge said, turning sharply toward her.

"No, no, of course not. He'd already figured most of it out. I just filled in the last details."

"Such as my killing that old man, I assume."

"That was an accident! That wasn't you. And I've explained how we've suppressed the violent tendencies that presented the first time you experienced the transformation."

Feverbridge continued to look from one to the other. He seemed to be experiencing a strange mix of emotions: surprise, alarm, hostility, and—what Logan sensed most strongly—anticipation.

"Father, there's a chance he can help."

"How can he help?" And Feverbridge took a seat on one of the lab stools. "We've been working to reverse this for half a year now—without success." He glanced out the open front door of the lab. "You have to leave now—both of you. I . . . I can't bear to be seen during these times. Go, please."

Instead, Logan casually sat down on a lab seat across from the older scientist. "Laura has told me you've managed to at least mitigate the effects," he said. "Locking yourself in, keeping moonlight to a minimum. But I'm curious: what does it feel like? When the change comes over you, I mean."

Feverbridge was silent a moment. "Discomfort. The pain is almost unbearable at first. Your skin, it . . . I don't know how to describe it. But one also feels a certain . . . energy. But it isn't a human strength—not exactly. It's a physical sensation merely, id without intellect."

"And the violence? Where does that emotion, that need, come from?"

"Laura told you," Feverbridge said brusquely. "That has been ameliorated. I prefer not to think about that—time."

"When you showed me that demonstration with the shrews—why were you unaffected?"

"I stood behind the light source—remember? It was trained directly on the animals: nowhere else."

"But if you were to train it on yourself, you'd undergo the transformation?"

"I suppose so, yes, if the light was of sufficient intensity. But as we've told you, I've done everything I can to shield myself from the full moon." He shifted impatiently on his seat. "I fail to see how this is in any way helpful to me."

"It's helpful to me, Dr. Feverbridge—in understanding exactly what's been going on. I have just a few more questions. Tell me: why do you think you have made so little progress in reversing your condition? After all, six months is a long time to work on the problem."

"If I knew that, perhaps we'd be making more progress than we have. There was something wrong with my initial hypothesis of how the imaginal discs would respond, such as those present in the metamorphosis of a caterpillar. I synthesized them to operate on a human scale and coded them to denaturate and reverse the transformation process. Instead, they seem to have bonded to my DNA, modified it. Trying to undo that modification is a process of trial and error—and dangerous if not done very carefully."

"Every time we seem to make a breakthrough," Laura said, "it turns out to be just another dead end."

"Are you willing to let others—other scientists, I mean—help you?" Logan asked. "Work with you?"

Feverbridge laughed bitterly. "If they didn't lock me up for killing that old man, they'd put me in a cage, point at me, *experiment* on me. And the scientific community that laughed at me all these years—think of what they'd say! Instead of seeing what I've accomplished, they'd see only failure: an inability to restore what I've changed."

"So you insist on staying here, working on this alone," Logan said.

Feverbridge gave a vigorous nod. "There's no other way. Laura's the only help I need."

That was it, then. Logan paused a moment, collecting his

thoughts. "Watching what happened to Zephraim Blakeney last night—well, it was a revelation, something that I will never forget, either professionally or personally. But there's something else that sticks with me—something that his brother Nahum said. You see, I asked him why—if the effect of the moon-sickness was so painful—did Zephraim pry the wooden planks from his window, deliberately exposing himself directly to the rays of the full moon? Nahum told me, as best he could understand, that—despite everything—Zephraim was drawn to the moon. He called it a craving. He said that it gave Zephraim a feeling of power, animalistic power. You alluded to something similar just now, although you used the euphemism of 'energy.' "

"Get to the point," Feverbridge said. He had slid down off his chair and was now pacing the lab, the very picture of impatience.

"It's just this: according to Laura, you reproduced the effects Zephraim experiences in yourself—except, thanks to the other accomplishments of your prior research, the result of your resequencing meant that you experienced the transformation on a far greater scale than Zephraim did."

Feverbridge did not answer; he simply continued pacing.

"So doesn't it stand to reason that you are drawn to the full moon all that much more—that you crave its light, crave the power it confers on you?"

"That's not so!" Laura protested.

"This 'energy' you mention—I imagine it's more like a well, something that you can tap almost at will. I can only imagine what that feels like."

"This is crazy!" Laura said. "My father is humiliated, sick at heart by what's happened, he—"

"That power, that craving—why would anybody want to have it taken away from them?" Logan asked Feverbridge. "I'd think just the opposite: they'd want to hold on to it any way they could. That's why you dazzled me by demonstrating your *earlier* research—the research on moon dust—knowing I would not turn you in, but rather, in my ignorance, let you proceed with what now *truly* interested you—the end you'd always hoped for, but had never been able to achieve . . . until the Blakeneys came along." He paused. "All these breakthroughs Laura mentions, the ones that turn out to be dead ends—did you engineer things so they would turn out that way? Is it possible the phenomena affecting you are becoming stronger, rather than weaker? That you are, in fact, *addicted* to the transformation—and this addiction maintains you through your calmer moments, preventing you from truly finding some way to undo what you've caused?"

"No!" Feverbridge cried in a hoarse voice.

"What is it you really do here by yourself, Dr. Feverbridge?" Logan pressed. "When you lock yourself in on the nights of the full moon, refusing to be seen even by your daughter. Are you really cowering in that back room, in the dark, with the tar paper covering the window?"

"Jeremy," Laura said, her tone changing abruptly. "What are you saying?"

"And that initial violent aspect of the transformation, the one you so conveniently managed to cancel out—even though you've made no other progress on your condition—is it *really* gone? Or is that what you've just led your daughter to believe? Because in my job as enigmalogist, I have to suspend my disbelief again and again, take a lot of things for granted—but one thing I never take for granted is coincidence. And the coincidence of your injecting yourself with that resequenced DNA, and the murders starting to take place shortly thereafter, is just a little too strong for me to accept."

As they had been speaking, darkness had gathered around the laboratory. At that moment, a stripe of moonlight suddenly drifted through the open door—and fell directly on Feverbridge.

"You son of a bitch!" he roared in a strangled voice. "You tricked me!"

Even as he spoke, Logan saw a strange pigmentation begin to spread across the skin of his exposed throat, blossoming like brown food coloring dropped into a basin of water. Feverbridge clutched at his neck, making gargling sounds, and blood-filled weals began to appear on his fingers and the backs of his wrists. He twisted, first this way, then that—and then he dashed out the door and into the darkness beyond.

"Father!" Laura cried out in shock and pain. She rounded on Logan. "My God, what have you done to him—"

"Stay here!" he cried. Then, running out of the lab and slamming the door behind him, he hurried up the path to the main complex. He was just in time to see the shadow of Feverbridge dart past the headlights of the red pickup truck that was now pulling into the fire station.

"Looks like I got here just in time," Albright said, getting out of his truck. "In the call you made earlier, you did say to arrive at moonrise." He reached into the front seat, pulled out his rifle. "I knew when you saw me loading this up that I'd hear from you, sooner or later. When you asked me to meet you at the Feverbridge lab, I assumed we were talking about the dogs. But that was no dog that ran in front of my headlights just now."

Logan did not reply. Instead, he ran to his Jeep, opened the glove compartment, and pulled out his own 9mm Sig Sauer. Then he rushed back to Albright.

"Come on," he said, gesturing in the direction Feverbridge had gone. "We don't have a moment to lose."

37

They began racing down the gravel path toward the highway. Already, Feverbridge had vanished into the darkness ahead.

"What happened?" Albright asked as they ran. "Were you right—about what you mentioned when you called me, I mean?"

"It's even worse than I thought," Logan replied. "The resynthesized serum wasn't administered to the dogs. Feverbridge gave it to himself."

"Are you saying that was him who ran in front of my truck just now? But he died six months ago."

"No. He killed a backpacker six months ago, a loner nobody would miss. Threw him off the top of Madder's Gorge. His daughter Laura misidentified the body to make people think Feverbridge was dead, so the scientific community who'd always scoffed at his work would leave him in peace—that was her explanation, anyway. Ever since, she told me, they've been trying to find a way to reverse the effects of what he did to himself."

"Which was what, exactly?"

"Inject himself with a highly potent and hybrid strain of Zephraim's moon-sickness."

"Holy shit. How did he do that?"

"I don't know all the details. I assume he modified a DNA sequence to introduce new genetic code into his genome—a single gene, or more likely a series of genes. In essence, he managed to simulate the effects of a multifactorial inheritance disorder."

"A what? How is that even possible?"

"It's the other cornerstone of his research: introducing a mutation into otherwise normal genetic code, specifically to cause metamorphosis. But we can worry about the details later. Because the most important thing is that he's not reverting to his old self, as he'd originally intended—if anything, he's getting worse. He's behind the four recent murders, and he seems to be getting more violent all the time."

They reached the road and paused for a moment. "Should we call in the cavalry?" Logan asked as he checked to make sure a cartridge was in the chamber of his gun.

"You mean, Krenshaw? It would take him forty-five minutes to get here."

"What about those troopers down the road, guarding the Blakeney compound?"

"It would take ten minutes to get *them*. And they'd just get in the way, slow us down. The longer we delay, the more chance Feverbridge has of killing again. Look, we've got a fresh trail to follow—and I can see it from here." With his torch, Albright pointed across the road, where some brush had been torn free from the surrounding tree limbs.

Albright rushed across the road and plunged into the woods on the far side, Logan at his heels. With the aid of Albright's torch, and the light of the full moon, they made their way through a maze of branches and heavy brush. More than once, Logan stumbled over an exposed tree root, protruding invisibly from the forest floor.

"It's a herd path of sorts," Albright said. "He's been this way before."

Now they entered a dense section of woods literally choked with pines. Logan forced his way forward, following Albright, who had slowed slightly in order not to lose Feverbridge's track. The heavy pine needles scraped along Logan's limbs as he pushed through them. Once, Albright lost the trail and they had to backtrack until he found it again. The pine forest descended into a muddy gully, which they splashed through before climbing the far bank. Suddenly, they broke free of the forest and found themselves on the remains of an ancient railroad, small trees growing up from between its rotting ties. It ran left and right, rails rusted and half covered in weeds, the screen of trees encroaching on both sides.

"What is this?" Logan asked, panting for breath.

"Private railroad," Albright answered. "Rail was once the primary mode of transport, both for passengers and freight. Back in the late nineteenth century, there were dozens of operators. Died out in the thirties with the automobile. I think this was the Adirondack and Lake Champlain." He knelt over the crumbling tracks, which shone an eerie yellow in the moonlight. "Look," he said, pointing to a pair of ragged, muddy footprints. "They're heading west, toward Desolation Mountain." He took some of the mud between his fingers, rubbed it carefully. "This has been here less than five minutes. Seems like we're gaining on him."

"That hardly seems likely—" Logan began, but Albright was already running down the tracks, his rifle—slung over his back—bouncing crazily between his shoulder blades.

Logan dashed after him. Albright had at least twenty-five years on him, but nevertheless he found it hard to keep up. Jogging along the abandoned rail line proved more difficult than he'd expected: the ties were spaced at just the wrong distance for running, and the interstices were full of brambles, weeds, and treacherous sinkholes.

The muddy tracks grew fainter, and Albright slowed accordingly, but he did not stop. Now and then he would lance his torch left or right, shining it over the unbroken flanks of forest that threatened to engulf the line.

After about a quarter of a mile, Albright came to a dead halt. He shone his torch around more slowly and carefully, scanning the dark woods. "There," he said after a minute, pointing to the left side of the tracks toward a stand of American beech. Logan had no idea what Albright had picked up, but he dutifully followed the man as he went tearing into the woods. Up ahead, he thought he could faintly make out the sound of crashing. His grip tightened around the handgun. He wondered for a moment what they would do if they caught up with Feverbridge—and then, almost immediately, he realized he already knew.

They scaled a height of land, then came out into a tiny clearing, ringed on all sides by beech. Ahead, rising above bare branches maybe half a mile away, was another fire tower—but unlike the one at the research site, this one appeared to be intact. It was a vast metal skeleton, perhaps two hundred feet tall, with a covered room at the top and a fire-escape-style ladder that switch-backed up its center from bottom to top. But Albright had taken off again, and Logan could not pause to examine it further.

"Phelps Fire Observation Station," Albright said over his shoulder. "Abandoned, of course."

Crossing the clearing, the moon above them bright with a surrounding swath of clouds, they entered the woods on the far side. Logan could no longer hear any sound ahead. Despite the occasional slowdown or false lead, he was truly impressed by Albright's knowledge of woodcraft. Whether through the tutelage of his father, Nahum Blakeney, his own youthful experience, or a combination of all three, he was somehow able to follow a trail that, to Logan, looked invisible.

The stand of beech gave way once again to pine, even thicker than before. "Strange," Albright said, stopping to examine a newly broken branch at shoulder height, fragrant with sap. "He's circling around to the south. It's almost as if he's doubling back—"

And at just that moment there came a sudden burst of sound to their right; the pine trees shook violently; and a creature of nightmare exploded out of the forest and onto them.

38

Laura Feverbridge stood in the doorway of the hidden lab. For a moment, she gathered herself to run after the others, but she remained immobile; it was as if the shocks of the last several minutes had left her paralyzed. She heard the sound of running footsteps, quickly receding; the squeal of brakes; a brief, urgent conversation—and then, silence.

Now, slowly, she turned around and walked back into the main room of the lab. Logan's insinuations—*accusations*—were crazy. She had worked with her father for months, trying to reverse the effects of the serum. True, most of the work had been done by her father—that was necessary, since she had to maintain a presence in the primary lab during the day, with the two lab assistants—but she'd seen enough of his work, helped with enough of it. He couldn't, wouldn't, deceive her—not after the sacrifices she'd made for him.

"Father," she murmured. "What have they done to you?"

At first, her steps had been slow, faltering, like a sleepwalker's, as she wandered aimlessly from table to table. But the more she thought about this awful turn of events, the more agitated her movements became. What to do? What to do?

There had to be something she could do.

This was the worst development imaginable. She'd trusted Logan, let him in on their secret . . . and he had betrayed her. Worse, he'd betrayed her father. God knew what he would do with that knowledge. But there was one thing she was certain of: these kind of gross accusations, on top of all the scorn her father had endured already, would have the worst possible effect on him.

As she paced, her eye fell on the door to his private room—the room where he did his own research, where she was forbidden to go.

She stopped. *Of course*. There would be proof in there; proof that he was doing his best to undo the dreadful affliction he was suffering, that this talk of his efforts being nothing but pretense was the vilest kind of slander.

She walked toward the door, hesitating slightly; to enter it felt like a violation, but she was doing so for the best of reasons. After a moment, she stepped through the door. It was furnished with surprising spareness; there was a cot, a sink, a table, and a rack of equipment—but the equipment was simplistic, almost meager; not the kind one would work with to solve this knotty a problem. Of course, he hadn't asked for anything particularly exotic— naturally, she'd ordered everything herself—but she'd assumed he'd taken what he needed from the main room of the secret lab and then returned it when he was done. She hadn't kept close tabs on what equipment was on hand at any one moment. . . . After all, he was her father, the senior scientist. . . .

Had he done most of his work in the main lab? Was this room the equivalent, perhaps, of a monk's cell, where he went to think, perhaps do trivial experiments—and suffer through the nights of the full moon, safely under lock and key?

Her eye fell on a lab journal, covered in green cloth, that lay on the table. The relief that flooded through her as she saw this caused her to realize just how distraught Logan's assertions had made her. Her father's private journal! This was exactly the proof she needed. It would contain a record of the attempts he'd made, the things he'd tried, what had been promising and what had not.

She snatched it up from the table and began paging through it quickly. But after only a minute, she stopped. A look of horror came over her face as she stared at the open page.

"*No,*" she whispered.

With trembling hands, she turned another page; read briefly; turned another . . . and then let the book drop to the floor.

And now, with no more hesitation, she left the room and ran toward the building's front door.

39

Logan felt himself go cold at the apparition that now confronted them among the thick pines. It was, without a doubt, Chase Feverbridge—but a Feverbridge who had become an abomination of nature.

He seemed to tower over them, his six-foot-four height increased by some trick of the moonlight. His white hair was matted and caked with dirt, full of twigs and dead leaves. His skin had become a blotchy mahogany color, studded here and there with pustulant boils, and it exuded a foul, animalistic odor, sour and musky. Patchy woolen hair covered his limbs. His mouth hung open avariciously. Huge hands, with long, spadelike, chitinous nails, flexed and clenched. Powerful muscles rippled beneath the woolen shirt. Worst of all were the small red eyes that stared at them with a mixture of hatred and hunger. Logan had seen eyes like those once before: in an emergency ward, where a youth suffering a bad PCP trip was being wheeled in by the staff. The youth had been screaming and frothing at the mouth, and—though a cop had hit him in the arm with a nightstick, causing a compound fracture—he was swinging the exposed bone around like a weapon, heedless of the pain, trying to gouge the orderlies who were rushing him into the hospital.

The ghastly spectacle was like a mindless, violence-mad travesty of Zephraim Blakeney—but an order of magnitude worse. Gone was the diffident man of science; in its place stood a creature of violent needs and animal lust. The feeling of wrongness, of nature twisted and perverted, washed over Logan like a wave.

All this took place in a split second. Then Albright began to free his rifle from his shoulder. With a roar, Feverbridge leapt forward and—with a single blow of a taloned hand—rent Albright from collarbone to sternum. Albright cried out with the pain, but still struggled to free his rifle. Feverbridge reached out and grabbed Albright's arm, gave it a vicious wrench; there was a *pop* like a cooked chicken leg being pulled from its carcass, and the arm dangled at a strange angle from the poet's shoulder, dislocated. Albright screamed in pain just as Feverbridge leapt on top of him, hand raised and fingers splayed wide, readying himself for the killing blow.

Logan realized that he had been instinctively backing up in horror during this one-sided battle. Now he raised his handgun and fired, winging Feverbridge in the shoulder. The man roared out, but remained fixated on the fallen Albright. Logan fired again, this time hitting Feverbridge in the leg. Now the man straightened up, howling in pain. Logan fired a third and fourth time, but his hand was shaking and the shots went wide. Feverbridge tensed himself, preparing to spring, and Logan—without a moment's additional thought—turned and ran for his life.

He tore mindlessly through the thick pine forest, heedless of the direction he was headed or obstacles in his path, aware of only one thing—the terrific crashing and snapping of branches behind him that made it horrifyingly obvious he was being pursued. He'd hit Feverbridge twice, but the shots hadn't slowed him down—at least, not by much. The man's plan was now all too clear. Albright had been correct about the unnaturally slow progress Feverbridge had made as he was being tracked, about how he was apparently doubling back on himself: despite his maddened state, he was aware that the two of them knew too much about him—and so he had laid a trap, waiting to ambush and kill them both.

Logan ran and ran, oblivious to the pine needles that raked his face and the branches that tugged at his limbs. Once he stumbled, but somersaulted forward back onto his feet and kept going without interruption, aware that at any moment he might feel those frightful nails tear across his back.

All of a sudden, the trees parted and a structure reared up ahead of him, spectral in the moonlight: the Phelps Fire Observation Station. The crashing sounds were still coming on, but he seemed to have put some distance between himself and Feverbridge. If he could get to the observation building at the top, he could use it as a blind and shoot Feverbridge when he came into the clearing. Immediately, he ducked between the metal struts that made up the sides of the tower and began climbing, two at a time, the exposed stairs that rose between them.

He made the first landing, started up the second switchback, then the third, before he heard a maddened roaring from below. A patch of thin clouds was now passing over the moon, but he could still make out the form of Feverbridge, crouching at the edge of the clearing below him. He half limped, half leapt for the staircase and began climbing with frenzied speed.

With something like despair, Logan realized he had made a tactical error. He still had two more switchbacks to go before reaching the top—he'd never make it in time. He pointed his gun at the climbing Feverbridge, squeezed off a shot—but the man-beast shrank away and the bullet ricocheted harmlessly off metal. He shot again, and this time Feverbridge grunted as the bullet bit through part of an ear—but it did not slow his frantic climb.

Logan looked around in desperation. There was only one chance. Without giving himself time to reconsider, he leapt from the open staircase onto the metal skeleton that made up the external structure of the station. He hit it with a bone-jarring impact; one hand slipped off the metal framing, but he quickly grasped it again. There was a bellow of anger from below and to one side. Ignoring this as best he could, Logan maneuvered his way crab-like along the beam until he reached a corner strut, then began sliding his way as quickly as he dared back down to the ground.

A terrific bang overhead told him that Feverbridge had duplicated his maneuver.

He hit the ground with a dreadful thump, then raced across the narrow clearing and reentered the pine forest, hoping against hope that Feverbridge had not seen the direction in which he'd run.

Another nightmarish dash through the pine forest began. Logan's sides were burning, and his ankles hurt from the heavy landing he'd just endured, but desperation lent new strength to his limbs. Once again, the crashing noises started up behind him, and with dismay Logan realized he had not ditched Feverbridge, after all.

He lost track of time, entering a kind of trancelike state in which all his concentration was bent on escape. He veered sharply, first left and then, a few hundred yards later, right; he was aware of tripping over another exposed root and falling flat on his face in the pine needles, losing precious time. The pain in his side became like fire, and each intake of breath was a small agony. But the frenzied bellowing from behind, the snapping noises of branches being thrust violently aside, forced him on.

. . . And then the trees fell away behind and he found himself on the top of a rocky outcropping, boulder-strewn flanks stretching away to the left and right. Nearby a stream bubbled up out of the rocks, falling away over the edge of the cliff and forming a waterfall that crashed onto the stones far below. Logan looked around as he gasped for breath. Although the clouds were still thickening, the light of the full moon was unimpeded, and it lit up the landscape below and beyond with a spectral illumination. Logan knew this spot: he was standing atop Madder's Gorge, where Feverbridge had first killed the lone backpacker, half a year before.

A snapping of twigs behind him and Feverbridge emerged from the shadow of the trees. With a low snarl of triumph, he leapt forward. Logan raised the gun but Feverbridge swatted it away with the back of his hand and it went tumbling over the cliff. Logan stepped backward as Feverbridge advanced. He was bleeding from the gunshot wounds; two had merely grazed him, but the third had clearly been a direct hit to his left thigh. Despite the extremity of his own situation, Logan couldn't help but marvel at the man's ability to cover ground so quickly, given a wound like that.

A half smile formed on Feverbridge's distorted mouth, and the little red eyes glowed with victorious malice. The hand that had swatted away the gun clenched into a fist; it came smashing down on Logan's shoulder with unbelievable strength and Logan immediately crumpled to the ground. Now the fist opened, fingers flexing as before, nails gleaming in the moonlight. With a howl of bloodlust, Feverbridge raised his arm, preparing to tear out Logan's throat.

Even as he did so, out of the night came a sudden, shouted word of command:

"Stop!"

40

Logan glanced over. It was Laura Feverbridge, advancing on them, moonlight glinting off the shotgun in her hands. In his preoccupation, struggling with the thing that had been Laura's father, Logan had not noticed her approach.

Feverbridge, too, turned toward her with a snarl. He advanced a step, snarling again. But then it seemed that recognition burned its way through the madness that had overtaken him, because he raised a hand over his face—perhaps to shield himself from Laura's terrible expression, perhaps to prevent her from fully seeing the change that had come over him. He retreated, one step, then another, and then his foot slipped on the edge of the cliff. He reared forward away from the edge as a group of thicker clouds began to scud across the bloated moon.

"You lied to me," she told her father in a voice choked with anger, betrayal, and grief. "After all the effort, all the deception, all I've done for you—you've been lying the whole time." She brushed away a tear with an angry gesture. "I found the journal in your private lab. I read your notes. Jeremy was right. Instead of trying to find an antidote, you've been secretly working to concentrate the serum—and you've been reinjecting yourself with it. Whenever we found a promising new avenue of research, you've paid lip service to the advance, pretending to be excited—and then you've subtly managed to undermine it. Every time. When I think of the hours, days, months I spent, worrying about you, trying to help you—all wasted, totally *wasted*!"

Logan tried to rise, realized from the sharp pain in his shoulder that it had been broken by the single, brutal blow from Feverbridge, and sank back. Feverbridge himself had gone still, staring at Laura. Exactly how much he could understand in his current state, Logan could not be sure—but he sensed the man-thing comprehended most, if not all, of what she said.

"And Jeremy was right about the other thing, wasn't he? You don't see what's happened to you as an affliction—you've started to *enjoy* it. All those full moons you said you spent locked in your private room so I wouldn't be burdened with the sight of your transformation—that violent impulse you said we managed to nullify after you murdered an innocent man in this very spot—those were lies, too. Weren't they? *Weren't they?*" Her whole body trembled with emotion; the shotgun shook in her hands. "And what's even worse, the killings have been accelerating. They aren't months apart anymore—they're *days*. You killed those two hikers. You killed our very own lab assistant. You killed the ranger, Jessup, who'd begun to have suspicions of his own. Each murder more brutal than the last. And now you're trying to kill Jeremy, as well—Jeremy, who only wanted to help!"

Suddenly, she raised the shotgun and pointed it directly at her father, openly weeping. "You've murdered five people. And that's all you want to do now—kill again. Oh, my dear God, what kind of position have you put me in? What choice have you given me? No choice at all!"

The moon was now fully covered by clouds; Madder's Gorge was reduced to a blue-black outline, illuminated by the palest ivory haze. As Logan watched, the madness in Feverbridge's eyes seemed to waver and lessen. The mahogany hue of his skin began to shrink, grow paler. *Maybe now I can get through to him,* he thought. *Maybe now he will listen.* Laura had the shotgun trained on her father, but she seemed unable—or unwilling—to pull the trigger.

"Dr. Feverbridge!" Logan shouted.

After a minute, Feverbridge turned from Laura to him.

"We know the truth now—all of it. This can't go on. Will you let us help you? Can you stop yourself, work to undo what you've become? Or are you going to keep on killing innocent people to satisfy an ever-growing bloodlust? Or . . . are you going to force your own daughter to kill you?"

As Logan spoke, Feverbridge stood motionless, like a statue. The red light died away in his eyes. The sense of wrongness, of nature perverted, that Logan had sensed emanating from him eased. He seemed to be wrestling with a deep inner conflict. He opened his mouth, but it was a low whine, not words, that came forth. He turned back toward Laura, her shotgun still pointed, tears streaming down her face, and his expression softened. He lifted one hand, reaching for her almost tenderly. At the same time, he took one quick step backward, then another—and then disappeared over the face of the cliff.

41

"Father!" Laura cried. The shotgun dropped from her hands, clattering forgotten onto the stones, and she turned and began scrambling down the path along the edge of the cliff. Even in the dim light, Logan could see that she was dashing along the trail at an almost suicidal pace, taking desperate chances as she leapt over rocks and fissures in an attempt to get to the bottom of the waterfall as quickly as possible. He rose to his feet and—doing his best to ignore the sharp pain in his shoulder—followed. By the time he reached her, she was at the edge of a little pool at the base of the cliff, water cascading all around, cradling the battered body of her father in her arms. She bent her head over him, weeping more loudly now.

With the absence of moonlight, Chase Feverbridge had

reverted to his normal self. Gone was the thick hair from his limbs; gone were the hoary, oversized nails. The battered form was once again the bemused, charismatic scientist he had first met in the secret lab, mere weeks before.

Looking on, he understood what had just happened. Feverbridge had seen the unmistakable pain in his daughter's eyes. He must have realized he was a lost soul. What he was doing was unpardonable—but it was something he could not stop, a murderous obsession that was only growing worse. Whether his daughter would have managed to shoot him, nobody could now say—but rather than force her to live with doing so, and knowing he could no longer change, he'd saved her from the terrible choice by taking his own life, falling from the top of the cliff—ironically, dying in exactly the way Laura said he had half a year earlier.

Logan pulled out his cell phone, dialed 911—it took three tries before he managed to keep the call from dropping—and gave them the location, as best he could, of where Albright could be found. Then he knelt beside her. She was rocking her father's head in her arms now, the weeping reduced to racking sobs.

"How did you know to come here?" he asked her gently.

It took her some time to answer. "I couldn't think where else to go."

He waited, perhaps ten minutes, perhaps fifteen, for the sobbing to stop. There was nothing more to say. Finally, he put a hand on her shoulder. "Come on. I'll take you back to the camp. Then we'd better call Krenshaw, turn ourselves in before he makes his move on the Blakeneys."

At this she looked at him for the first time since he'd come up beside her. "Turn ourselves in? You've done nothing wrong. If anything, you were the one who came here tonight and showed me the truth. If it wasn't for you, he'd have killed again. And again, and again. I'm the one—the only one—at fault. I wanted to believe him. I thought I *did* believe him. But deep down, I guess I always wondered—was he really there, locked in that room of his, on the nights of the full moon? Why was it that our research kept running into blind alleys? I should have asked myself those questions directly. Despite his pleas for privacy, to respect his affliction, I should have looked in on him those nights when the moon was full. I realize now the reason I never did was because I didn't . . . didn't want to know the truth." She sniffed. "I thought I could cure him. But all I did was prolong his murderous obsession. And now, because of me—directly or indirectly, it doesn't matter—four more people have died."

And with this she laid her father's head gently on a rock, rose, turned, and began walking back in the direction of the fire station. Logan watched her receding form for a minute until it was nothing more than a phantom, gray against black. And then he, too, rose from the gurgling pool and, moving slowly and painfully, began to follow.

Two months later, Logan was scheduled to attend a conference of medieval historians in Quebec. At the last minute, he canceled his flight and decided to drive instead—although it was now December, the weather was warm and no snow was expected. As he drove up the Northway—and then, well before the Canadian border, took the exit that led to NY Route 73—he was aware of two distinct and very different memories of this particular trip: the ones he'd taken with his wife years before, and the very different one he had made this past October.

He did not want that latter memory to be the one that remained uppermost in his mind. And so he very purposefully made the drive past Keene, Lake Placid, and Saranac Lake, turning first onto Route 3, and then 3A, reliving events both new and old. Save for the stands of pine, the trees were completely bare now, and even in the densest woods he could see the clear blue sky above. The secondary roads were as bad as ever, and just occasional patches of snow could be seen here and there as he drove on deeper into the forest.

"Don't worry, Kit," he murmured. "Two hours, tops, and then we'll be back on the freeway again."

As he steered the Elan around the curves, he allowed himself—gingerly—to get a sense of the woods around him. There was no longer a feeling of malice, or a perversion of the proper order of things. The Adirondacks remained imperially indifferent to the little humans who hiked and worked and moved within them, but it now felt like a benign indifference to Logan. Man would come and till the fields and lie beneath, but nature would go on regardless.

He turned in at the driveway beside the A-frame, parked next to the red pickup, made his way along the front path, and knocked on the door. It was opened a few moments later by Harrison Albright.

"You're late," the poet said.

"Sorry. Didn't start as early as I'd planned. Never do."

"Well, come in, anyway."

Logan followed the man into the rustic living room. Albright moved a little stiffly, but evidently his wounds had by and large healed.

The poet sat him down in one of the handmade chairs, then produced two mugs of coffee with—at his insistence—a good splash of bourbon in each. They lounged before the crackling fire, sipping and saying nothing, for several minutes.

"I was a little surprised to get your call," Albright said finally.

"Why?"

"I would have thought you'd seen enough of this place to last a lifetime."

"Don't worry, this is as far as I go. No need for another visit to Pike Hollow. But . . ." Logan paused. "I couldn't leave it like that."

Albright nodded his understanding.

"And I also wanted to thank you, face-to-face, for all your help."

This produced a dismissive wave.

"Also, I was curious about what's happened since I left. Nobody's told me anything, of course. But I figured if anybody knew the story, it would be you."

Albright took a sip of coffee. "It's true, I have my sources. But I really haven't heard all that much, either. Apparently, it's being treated as a unique case. It was taken away from Krenshaw immediately and referred higher up the chain of command. There was even talk of the CDC getting involved."

"Not with the Blakeneys, I hope."

Albright shook his head. "Nobody's touched the Blakeneys— and nobody will. It's like we promised them: what we saw in that compound will stay in that compound."

"Of course." The enigmalogist in Logan felt this was a shame: not studying the unique "moon-sickness" of the clan, and adding the resultant findings to the body of medical knowledge, seemed a missed opportunity. The humanist in him, however, knew that the Blakeneys had suffered enough from unwanted attention, gossip, and open hostility over the years and that they deserved to be left alone.

"What about Laura Feverbridge?" he asked at last.

"From what I've heard, she's being treated lightly. She was an indirect accomplice to what happened—but an accomplice to something nobody could have anticipated or understood. I believe she'll get off with probation."

"An indirect accomplice," Logan said, hearing the bitterness in his own voice.

Albright raised his eyebrows inquiringly.

Logan sighed. "Usually, when I finish a case, I'm able to put it behind me. Walk away. Even those that I don't solve, can't find a satisfactory solution to, don't linger to disturb my dreams. But this one . . . this one was different. *Is* different."

"You're upset by the role you played in it," Albright said.

"Precisely. Imagine someone—someone very much like myself—stumbling on the fact that Dr. Feverbridge hadn't died, after all. His daughter had come upon the body of a dead hiker, someone nobody would miss, and used that as an opportunity to hide her father away, free him from the academic scorn that had troubled him so much that he tried to commit suicide. Father and daughter plead with this someone to keep their secret. It's an innocent deception, he's told. Nobody was hurt by it. And so the someone agrees."

"Except that it turns out people *were* hurt. Five men were killed."

"And that's why the case doesn't want to fade away. I can't seem to shake the ethical dilemma of it; the results of my action—or inaction."

For a few minutes, the two fell silent, mutely sipping their coffee. At last, Albright shifted in his chair.

"You know," he began, "I almost hate to say it, but it seems to me that what you're describing would frequently be part of the baggage of a job like yours. When you study enigmas— when you immerse yourself in solving them—you just might find yourself walking out of the woods at the end of the day, enigma resolved . . . but with yourself now burdened by an ethical enigma of your own. Your friend Jessup might have told you to remember the famous words of Nietzsche."

Logan thought a moment. " 'If you stare into the abyss, the abyss stares back at you.' "

Albright's only response was to smile a little conspiratorially and take another sip of his coffee.

Logan held Albright's gaze for a long moment. And as he did so, he realized—with the faintest of shocks at not having realized it before—that the old woodsman was right.

Those who know the Adirondacks well will no doubt observe
that I have interspersed the names of real places with numerous
fictitious ones. Even the "real" locations I employ do not always
match their counterparts in the actual world. I have taken liber-
ties with the mountains, towns, hamlets, wilderness regions, history, and geography of the Adirondacks in order to suit the needs
of the novel, and the brooding setting of *Full Wolf Moon* is as
much a creation of my own whimsy as it is a direct reflection of
that vast and wonderful park.

　　While I tried to portray the duties and divisions of the New
York State Forest Rangers and New York State Police with a
degree of accuracy, all rangers, troopers, and state or federal
employees, etc., in *Full Wolf Moon* are fictitious and the products

of my imagination, and should not be considered to be a portrayal of any actual person or persons, living or dead.

I wish to thank my wife, Luchie, for reading the manuscript and making several excellent suggestions; Doug Preston, for suggesting the addition of "moon dust" to the novel; and my friend and editor, Jason Kaufman, for his guidance and companionship over many years of enjoyable literary toil together.

ABOUT THE AUTHOR

Lincoln Child is the #1 *New York Times* bestselling author of *The Forgotten Room, The Third Gate, Terminal Freeze, Deep Storm, Death Match,* and *Lethal Velocity,* as well as coauthor, with Douglas Preston, of numerous *New York Times* bestsellers, most recently *The Obsidian Chamber* and *Beyond the Ice Limit.*